Mouse Mountain

Phil Brown

Other books in the Mouse Mountain series:

Mouse City

Mouse World

ISBN-13: 9798362420710

For Angela and Stanley

1

An Evil Plot

'Dandelion! Can't you go any faster?'

Dan looked up from the steep, rocky path under his paws and found Hawthorn glaring back at him. Stupid little mouse! It was all right for him, he wasn't carrying anything. Dan had two heavy bags slung over his shoulders and he was sure their straps were rubbing bare patches in his fur.

He dropped the bags down onto the path, sending up puffs of dust, then sat down on one of them.

The other mouse shook his head. 'This is no time to rest, you know... we're nearly there.' And with that he turned away and scurried on up the path.

Dan watched him go. He really should get up and follow. He was meant to do everything Hawthorn told him to do, because Hawthorn was the senior apprentice and Dan was only the junior. But Dan wasn't very good at doing what he was supposed to do.

Up ahead Hawthorn was starting to look small in the distance, and... was he climbing up something? Some kind of rockfall blocking the path?

A shout drifted back down to Dan. 'Aha!' And Hawthorn disappeared.

Maybe they really were nearly there... wherever it was they were going.

Better get moving. Dan stood up and heaved the bags back onto his shoulders then started forwards again, carefully placing one paw in front of the other and avoiding any loose rocks. The path was very narrow and a huge river raged down to Dan's right. He didn't want to trip and fall in. He shivered at the thought. The churning water looked cold and dark and... hungry.

Trudge... trudge... trudge.

Why were they walking anyway? They were temple mice, and temple mice could shift... just visualise where they wanted to travel to, close their eyes, and... go there. But Hawthorn had insisted on walking the whole way – five days of trekking and sleeping out at night – and finally this long slog up a mountain path.

Dan reached the rockfall. Up close it looked bigger – twice his height and completely blocking the path. He glanced at the river, its strong current swirling eddies around the edge of the rockfall where it had slumped into the water. He took a deep breath. If Hawthorn could get over this thing, he could do it too. He started picking his way up, each step sending skitters of rocks and stones down to splash into the river, and when he got to the top he was surprised to see that the path beyond widened into a big, flat beach of stones and small rocks. Hawthorn was at the back of the beach, staring into a big, dark hole dug into the bottom of a grassy bank.

Dan skidded and slipped down the far side of the rockfall and called over. 'Where are we, Hawthorn?'

The other mouse snapped back impatiently. 'You don't need to know! Just wait here and don't do anything stupid.'

And without another word he disappeared into the blackness of the hole.

An hour later Dan was sitting on a flat rock staring at the river. He'd already explored the whole of the small beach and hadn't found anything remotely interesting. He'd also tried to skim stones on the fast waters of the river, which had turned out to be impossible. He'd even poked his head into the hole to see if he could see anything, which he couldn't.

And now he was bored.

He sighed to himself. What were they doing here anyway?

He was getting fed up with running around after Hawthorn. In fact, he was getting fed up with being an apprentice elder altogether.

The thought made his mind wander back to the ceremony in

the temple last year – when he and his friends had graduated. They'd been so excited. Finally it had been the end of three years of studying and training, and the end of being stuck in a temple on a mountainside in the middle of nowhere. They'd whispered and giggled while a lot of boring speeches had rolled on by. But then a big announcement had got their attention. Ragweed, the head elder, had stated grandly that for the first time in ten years a student had done well enough to have the honour of becoming an apprentice elder! Dan had clapped and cheered with everyone else and looked around wondering who it was. Then Ragweed had called out Dan's name!

Some honour! It had turned out to be a load more work. And a load more time stuck in the temple while his friends went off and got on with their lives.

Could he give up his apprenticeship? He imagined the shocked faces of the elders if he tried to. Had anyone ever dared do it before?

As he daydreamed, he stared into the river. It was wider here, but still deep, running fast with meltwater from the mountain peaks that loomed over the beach. His gaze moved to the far bank. It was made of smooth rock, with folds and hollows scoured by centuries of floodwater. He saw a pool of still water in one of the hollows. It looked cool and clear.

Dan's paws were sore from slogging up the rocky path. It would be good to dangle them in that pool. He shook his head at the idea. The river was too strong to cross.

But he could shift.

They'd walked all the way up here... but was there any reason he couldn't shift over to the other side of the river?

That pool looked so good.

He focused on the smooth rock next to the pool, then hesitated. Should he do this? Hawthorn would be cross. But... how would he ever find out? Dan willed himself to shift.

It started the same as always, with everything going black and Dan getting a feeling like he was floating... but then long seconds ticked by, more than usual. This wasn't right. Suddenly something grabbed him, like a huge hand round his whole body, and squeezed him until he could hardly breathe. Then it threw him. Hard.

Light exploded into his eyes and he had an instant to see the beach hurtling towards him – and then he was skidding along it, bouncing when he hit rocks and finally thudding into the bank next to the hole. He cried out as the wind was knocked out of him. 'Ooof!'

He lay there getting his breath back. Maybe he shouldn't have tried to shift. Was this why Hawthorn had insisted on walking up here?

He muttered as he pushed himself back onto his paws. 'That was a bad idea.'

Everything hurt. But after a few limping steps the pain eased a bit. He decided nothing was broken.

He looked around the beach with fresh eyes. Some serious

magic was going on here, stopping anyone shifting in or out of this place. Back at the temple they had something similar, but it didn't try to kill you! His gaze ended up on the hole that Hawthorn had disappeared into. What lived in there? He edged towards it and peered inside. It was inky black.

Dan took one step into the hole. Then a second step.

He paused to see if anything happened.

Nothing did.

He edged further and further into the absolute darkness.

Dan froze as his paw touched a loose rock and sent it clattering to the ground.

He'd been creeping forwards in the darkness for five minutes. A glow of light from somewhere up ahead had been slowly getting brighter – and a low murmuring rise and fall of voices had been getting louder.

But now the murmuring voices stopped suddenly.

He stood as still as he could – imagining ears up ahead listening for any slight sound. He held his breath and his nose felt like sneezing. The silence went on and on.

Until finally the voices started again.

Dan let out his breath slowly. What was he doing? If Hawthorn caught him he'd be furious. Dan started to turn back. But then five words sounded more loudly and clearly from the murmuring up ahead.

'.... temple will be completely destroyed!'

Dan froze again. Had he really heard that? Something about the temple being destroyed?

He started inching forwards again.

The light ahead grew stronger and the voices grew louder. More and more words became clear.

'... mountain...'

'... eruption...'

Dan came to a corner. The light and the voices seemed to be coming from just around the other side of it.

He leaned forward and peeped around the corner. And saw that the hole opened up into a chamber – about twenty paces across. The light was coming from a globe that was hovering in mid-air. Two heads were close in conversation over a table under the light, their bodies lost in shadows but Dan guessed they were sitting on cushions.

Dan recognised Hawthorn's voice.

'What about the legend of the cat?'

A deeper voice replied – it didn't sound like a mouse.

'Hmmm, yes, the cat.'

'Do you think it really exists?'

'Yes... I know it does.'

'It does? I thought it might just be a legend.'

'I thought so too. But I don't like to leave things to chance and so I spent a long time searching for that cat. And I found it. It's a long way from here – in a different world – I think it may have been hidden there on purpose.'

'There are different worlds?'

The deep voice chuckled. 'Many of them. You have a lot to learn. I'll show you – open your mind!'

The deep voice had such a note of command that Dan found himself obeying as well. As a student he'd learned how to open his mind to an elder – but this animal wasn't an elder! In his head a vision appeared of a track on a slope above a wide slow river. A grey cat was walking along the track. With the vision came a sense of place and time – of where that path was and when the cat would be on it. That place was so far away that he gasped.

The deep voice immediately shouted. 'Who is that?'

The vision was snatched back and the globe in the cavern flared with bright light. And Dan knew that he'd been caught!

Dan stepped out into the light.

'Dandelion!' Hawthorn exclaimed.

Dan knew he was in trouble now. Hawthorn glared at him.

'I told you to stay outside!'

Dan looked down. But then he looked up again and faced Hawthorn's stare – he was fed up with being ordered around by the skinny mouse.

The deeper voice of the other creature cut in. He didn't sound cross – merely curious. 'So this is the new apprentice?'

Dan looked at the creature. He was huge. Definitely not a mouse. Too tall and skinny to be a rat either. He might be a Weasel – Dan had heard of them, but never seen one before. He found himself asking. 'Are you a Weasel?'

The deep voice chuckled. 'You are a brave little mouse. Yes, I am a Weasel.'

'Oh.'

The Weasel spoke again – in a casual, dangerous sounding, voice. 'Do you know what Weasels eat?'

'Carrots?'

The Weasel chuckled again. 'Good try. But no, we eat rabbits, voles, birds, rats.... sometimes mice.'

Dan shivered. Why had Hawthorn brought them to see such a dangerous creature?

The Weasel carried on speaking – he seemed to be enjoying this. 'But I'm not hungry at the moment. So, little apprentice, please go back outside and wait for your master.'

There was a note of command in the Weasel's voice again that made Dan turn away and start to shuffle out. It took an effort of will to stop himself. He gathered his courage to speak again. 'Err... is the legend coming true... about the temple?'

The Weasel and Hawthorn both stared at him for long seconds. The Weasel licked his lips.

Hawthorn waved at him to leave with one paw. 'Just go and

wait outside. We'll discuss this later.'

This time Dan didn't hesitate. He was scared. He turned and scampered away down the tunnel away from the chamber.

When Dan was gone Hawthorn turned back to the Weasel.

'How much do you think he heard?'

'Enough to be a problem, I would say.'

'He will want to warn the others – he is close to the queen.'

'We will have to make sure he doesn't.'

'How? Can you make him forget?'

'Oh yes – permanently I think – just give me a moment.'

The Weasel closed his eyes and concentrated. Hawthorn was amazed – was it that easy to make someone forget something they'd overheard?

'There – that should solve the problem,' the Weasel opened his eyes again.

'And now – there are still a few things to plan.'

They sat down at the table again.

Dan kept banging his paws on rocks. The hole seemed even darker on the way out. His mind was buzzing. The temple might be destroyed? Memories flared of the walls in the great temple hall and the pictures carved onto them. Dan and his friends had spent a lot of time studying them when they were students. The best one had showed the temple being blown up by the mountain erupting. There were pictures of lava a. . . smoke and burning mice – it was great. But now Hawthorn and that Weasel thought it was really going to happen?

Finally he saw daylight ahead.

He came out onto the rocky beach blinking – and immediately stumbled to a halt. There were rats on the beach – ten of them at least. And they were all looking at him, as though they'd been waiting for him.

'Is that him, Mordred?' One rat said.

'Must be,' another rat replied. 'And call me 'sir''.

All the rats were bigger than Dan. But the one called Mordred was huge. He was nearly the size of a cat – it was unnatural.

'All right you lot,' the big rat ordered. 'Don't let him get away.'

The rats pulled out swords – they were rusty, dirty looking things – and started moving forwards. Mordred stayed at the back, watching.

Dan waited. There was no point trying to run. There were too many of them.

One of the rats got pushed forwards by the others.

'Go on Ember!' A voice hissed.

The rat hesitated for a second – he looked petrified – then he ran at Dan with his sword raised high. He swung the sword with all his strength. And a moment later found himself flying head-first into the Weasel's hole – without his sword.

Dan spun back round to face the rest of the rats, now holding

careful,' mentioned Mordred. 'He's a temple

more rats leapt forward. Dan ran between them. Sparks flew as Dan deflected both of their blades. Dan didn't stop – he kept on going into the middle of the group of rats – slashing with the rat sword as he went. Two rats fell down with cuts in their back legs – another squealed as its ear was chopped off. But then suddenly Mordred was in front of Dan and his great sword came down with a mighty swipe. Dan tried to stop the blow with his stolen rat sword but it shattered. Dan was lucky though. He had deflected Mordred's sword enough so that it didn't chop him in half – and only seared a long cut down his back. Dan dodged away and ran back the way he had come, his back hot with pain, expecting Mordred to follow – but the big rat didn't.

'Finish him off,' he heard Mordred say casually.

Dan was breathing heavily as he faced the rats again. He was back where he started with the Weasel's hole behind him. Except now he could feel blood dripping down his back. He started to feel dizzy – and wondered how bad his wound was.

He watched as the rats came forward again – more wary now – getting ready to rush him all at once. But they still hung back, and Hawthorn heard quiet footsteps behind him coming back out of the hole. The small rat again, he was sure, and the others were all waiting for him to jump on Dan from behind. The footsteps got closer and closer...

Now! He spun round and grabbed the small rat's outstretched paws, then ducked down and used its own momentum to throw it over his head.

There was a moment of confusion as the flying rat bowled into the others and Dan used it to dodge between them and scamper sideways across beach. If he could just get to the path, he was sure he could outrun the rats.

But the big rat called Mordred was too fast again and appeared out of nowhere to trip him up and send him sprawling face first onto the ground.

'Not bad,' the big rat rumbled.

A foot kicked him and Dan ended up on his back – with the rat standing over him.

'If you want a job doing – you have to do it yourself,' Mordred complained, and raised his huge sword to stab down at Dan's chest.

Dan had one chance – one last thing he could do to save himself. He closed his eyes and shifted, thinking of the pool across the river again. It was the only way to avoid being skewered – even if he did get grabbed and thrown again.

Everything went black.

Like last time there were a few moments of darkness and then Dan felt himself grabbed and thrown – and an instant later he was flying through the air again. But this time in front of him, instead of the stony beach, was a huge hairy back.

Mordred's sword clanged as it hit the stones where Dan had been lying, and he had just enough time to be surprised before being knocked flat on his face.

Smashing into Mordred slowed Dan down but he still found himself bouncing and skidding over the stones of the beach. But this time, to his horror, he saw he was tumbling towards the river and wasn't going to stop in time.

The sudden coldness of the rushing water was a shock. Dan scrabbled with his paws but there was nothing to grab. He was surrounded by cold wetness and could feel the force of the river dragging him along. For an instant his head came back above the surface and he grabbed a breath of air. He just had time to see the rats watching him from the shore before he was dragged back under.

Mordred pushed himself up from the ground.

'What happened?' He felt like he'd been charged by a raging badger.

'That mouse hit you from behind,' one of the rats said.

Mordred shook his head, that was one tricky mouse. 'Where is he?'

All the rats pointed at the river. One replied. 'He fell in there.'

Mordred walked down to the edge of the water. He scanned the opposite bank, then peered downstream. There was no sign of the mouse, but the river was running fast and deep. There was no way a mouse could survive in there. He put away his sword. 'All right, I suppose we got him, then.'

He was about to turn away from the river when he spotted something shining amongst the rocks near the water's edge. He bent down and picked it up. Of all things – it was a small golden key!

He smiled. The mouse must have dropped it – and he had a good idea what it was. He put it into a pouch in the belts he wore across his chest. Then he shouted to the rats. 'Okay you lot, line up and hold paws – let's get out of here!'

Injured rats were pulled up onto their paws and helped limping to the middle of the beach. Then all the rats stood in a line and held paws – three of them moaning in pain. Mordred took a black stone out of another pouch and considered it for a moment. It had been a gift from the Weasel. Cut into the shape of a diamond, it allowed him shift like the mice could do.

He didn't like it. He preferred to get about using his paws! But he was hundreds of miles from his army and this was the only quick way back. He grabbed the paw of the rat at the end of the line and then stared into the stone, concentrating hard on where he wanted to go. For a moment the stone became even blacker and Mordred felt the scary sensation of being sucked into it.

An instant later the rats had disappeared, and the beach was empty again.

Hawthorn came out of the hole late in the afternoon expecting to find Dan, but there was no one there. He looked around and found the shattered remains of a nasty looking sword amongst the rocks on the beach – and also dried bloodstains, and something that looked like a rat's ear. He glanced fearfully back at the hole in the bank as the truth hit him. The Weasel hadn't used magic to make Dan forget what he'd heard – he'd summoned his rats to kill him.

Hawthorn was scared. He had a deal with the Weasel, but what had happened to Dan made him realise just how ruthless the Weasel was.

He looked at the two bags on the beach and let out a huff of annoyance. Now he'd have to carry his own bag back!

He picked his bag up and left Dan's behind, then headed across the beach to the rockfall and the path back down by the river. As he went, he started to worry about how he was going to explain Dan's disappearance when he got back to the temple.

2

Saving Milly

The man was standing in a shallow part of a calm, wide river. He wore strange, long rubber boots that looked like trousers and was waving a long, thin stick backwards and forwards over his head.

Milly the cat sat on the bank of the river, fascinated by the line that flicked at the end of the man's fishing rod, skimming the surface and touching it sometimes, making the light of the afternoon summer sunshine glint on droplets of water. She leaned forwards with excitement when the line pulled down suddenly and licked her lips as the man pulled it slowly in, grabbing a fish from its end and dropping it into a big net that drooped into the river beside him.

Milly wished she could have that fish. She could almost taste it. One day she would steal a fish from the man – one day.

The man started wading back towards the shore – he was finished for the day. Milly had seen him catch three fish. She crouched down in the grass on the riverbank so he wouldn't see her. She lay as still as she could.

'Get out of it – you stupid cat!' A stone crashed close to where Milly was crouching. She jumped up and ran before the man could grab another stone from the riverbed to throw at her, not slowing down until she was out of range.

She walked away from the river along a narrow path that angled up a steep hill, so lost in a daydream about stealing fish that she didn't notice a rat standing in her way until she'd almost bumped into it.

'Oh!' She said.

It was a nasty looking thing. Black and skinny – but bigger than a rat should be – maybe half her size. She hissed at it, expecting it to run away. But the thing just bared its teeth and reached over its back to pull out a sword.

'Oh!' Milly said again.

'Is that all you can say?' The rat sneered. And with that it leapt at Milly, raising its sword over its head.

Milly had no time to react – and was too shocked to avoid the rusty blade – but the rat never reached her. A brown furry shape shot out from the grass at the side of the track and hit the rat in mid-air. They both disappeared as they rolled away down the slope towards the river.

Milly stood still for a second. The path in front of her was empty. It was as though she'd imagined the rat.

Then an urgent squeak came from somewhere down the slope.

'Run for it!'

Run? From what? Milly looked around her – and jumped out of her skin when she saw more rats scampering up the path from behind. Milly ran. It felt wrong, running away from rats. But they had swords. She ran as fast as she could.

Cats are a lot faster than rats. She started to leave them behind. But then another group of rats jumped out into the path ahead of her. There was no way she could stop. She jumped – and went right over their heads. They snarled in frustration. She heard them scrabbling around to follow her again and went even faster to get away from them. But then something else stepped out to block the path in front of her.

Milly dug her four paws into the ground to stop. This thing looked like another rat – but it was even more huge. It pulled out its own sword as she skidded along the path towards it.

'If you want a job doing...' it sighed.

She managed to stop just in time and swerve off the path.

She half ran, half tumbled, down through the long grass of the hillside back towards the river. She couldn't stop if she wanted to. About halfway down she saw she was heading for a big rock and jumped so that she'd miss it, but that threw her completely off her paws and the rest of the way she just crashed and rolled.

Milly ended up sprawled on the river's bank. She felt bumped and bruised – but at least she'd left those rats behind. She had just pushed herself up onto her paws when the air around her wavered and she was suddenly surrounded again.

'All right – let's finish this,' the huge rat ordered.

But before the rats could move a jagged stone came flying through the air and hit one them. It went tumbling backwards then lay still. For a moment they all stared at it in shock.

Then a big voice boomed. 'Blinking rats!'

Another stone hit one of the other rats a glancing blow that threw it sideways. Then another narrowly missed the huge rat. The rats turned and ran.

There was a huge laugh and rubber boots stomped past Milly. She looked up and saw the man who had been fishing.

'Bet you'd like one of these!' The man wafted his net of fish past Milly's nose as he went by.

He paused to kick the dead rat into the river – then carried on walking away along the riverbank. Milly watched him go.

A voice came from next to Milly, making her jump. 'They'll be back – we must get away!'

She looked down and saw a brown mouse – she guessed it was the brown furry shape that had saved her from the first rat. The mouse held out a paw to her.

'Think about somewhere safe – and take my paw.'

She stared at the paw – it was bigger than any mouse paw she had ever seen. The mouse was smaller than the rats, but not by much.

Milly was in shock and just did what the mouse told her to do – she thought about her house, up the hill from the river – and reached out her own paw to touch the mouse's.

Everything went black.

🐑 🐑 🐑

It was the weirdest thing that had ever happened to Milly. She felt like she was floating, like when you bounce on a trampoline and you get to the bit where you're as high as you're going to get but haven't started to come back down yet. Just like that... except that it went on and on.

'Help,' she whispered to herself.

She kept blinking her eyes, but it didn't make any difference whether they were open or shut, the blackness was the same. She started to feel sick.

Then suddenly it was light again and she was hovering just above her garden. She fell down onto the grass with a bump.

She got up onto her paws, looking around. There was her house, right in front of her, somehow. And there was the mouse, on the grass next to her, crouched low to the ground and not looking very well.

'Are you all right?'

'Not really.'

Milly looked at the mouse properly for the first time. It was brown – and was wearing an odd leather belt round its middle – and straps over its shoulders. It was soaking wet and shaking.

'Who are you?' She asked.

'I don't feel too good,' the mouse slumped down onto its side.

Milly saw blood on its back. 'Is that a cut?'

'Does it look bad?'

Milly nodded. 'Not great.'

'We need to hide,' the mouse said.

'Why? What's going on?' Milly was still scared. 'Why were those rats chasing me?'

'They want to kill you.'

'Oh!' Milly had kind of guessed that from the swords – but it was still a shock to hear the mouse say it. 'Why me?'

The mouse paused before answering. It was breathing heavily.

'It's a long story, there's no time – we need to hide – they won't stop 'til they get you.'

Its words came out in gasps.

Milly looked around nervously. The garden was surrounded by high fences but she could imagine rat heads popping over the top at any moment.

'All right – can you walk?'

The mouse closed its eyes and Milly poked it with her paw – it was still breathing but it didn't react.

'Oh great,' she murmured to herself.

She picked up the mouse carefully in her mouth and took it around the side of the house to her cat flap. She crept quietly through the house to avoid the family she lived with; they might start shouting if they saw her carrying a mouse. One of her favourite places to hide was the linen cupboard in one of the bedrooms. She took the mouse there and dropped it on some old towels at the back. The mouse didn't move. Was it dead? But then it sighed and gave a small snore.

She stared at it. What on earth was she going to do now?

She needed the mouse to get better so it could tell her what was going on.

It had better not die, she thought, or... she'd kill it!

3

Escape to the temple

Milly checked on the mouse every morning and evening for three days, worrying more and more that it always seemed to be asleep. What if it did die and started to smell?

Then on the fourth morning it was gone. She pulled all the towels out of the cupboard – but it definitely wasn't there. Typical, she thought, ungrateful mouse, gone without a single thank you. Then she heard an odd groaning sound. She looked up to where the noise was coming from and saw a dark brown paw hanging down over the top of the wardrobe.

'Ouch!'

That sounded like Boris, her brother. Her heart fell. Had he eaten the mouse?

'Is that you Boris?' She asked.

A brown cat's head peeped over the top edge of the wardrobe.

'Is it gone?'

'What?'

'The mouse.'

'Yes – it is.'

'Thank goodness.'

'What happened?'

'Nothing,' groaned Boris. 'I just came up here for a rest.'

'So you didn't eat the mouse?'

'No – I let it go.'

'Hmm.' That didn't seem likely to Milly.

Milly watched as Boris stretched and moaned some more. For all the world it seemed like he was a bit bruised. Milly shrugged and went to search for the mouse.

It wasn't anywhere in the house – so Milly's only choice was to start looking outside – where the rats might be waiting. She gathered her courage and crept out through the cat flap.

She scanned the garden. Nothing.

She crept out past the shed, crouching low to the ground, ready to dart back into the house at the first sight or sound of danger. But when a sound did come – it came from behind her. She was halfway down the path to the garden gate when a scrabbling noise made her spin round in fright – imagining rats, cutting off her escape route back to the cat flap.

But instead, what she saw was another cat. A tabby – big and tough – walking slowly towards her. He was the neighbourhood bully, Stripy. The sight of him sent a shiver of fright through Milly.

'What a nice surprise,' Stripy said nastily. 'Out here all on your own, without your brother.'

Something tugged Milly's tail. She looked round and saw the

mouse she'd been looking for. How had it got there? It whispered up to her. 'That cat doesn't seem very nice – why are you friends with it?'

'I'm not,' Milly whispered back.

'Well, well, well,' Stripy sat down a few paces away. 'A cat and a mouse.'

Stripy licked a paw.

'I met some rats today who are looking for a cat and a mouse,' he said lazily. 'It looks like I might be able to tell them where you are.'

'No, don't...' Milly pleaded.

'Don't?' Stripy repeated. 'Well, I might not.'

Stripy stood up. 'If I can eat your mouse.'

Without warning Stripy jumped forward. But Milly stood her ground and snarled.

'Out of my way!' Shouted Stripy, and with one swipe of his paw he knocked Milly head over paws.

Stripy laughed and pounced on the mouse.

But somehow he missed it.

Milly saw it dodge sideways faster than she had ever seen any mouse move and scurry around behind the big cat. Without pausing it leapt up to land on Stripy's head and leaned down to pull out two of the cat's whiskers.

'Ouch!' Said Stripy, rubbing at his face as the mouse somersaulted off his head to land in front of him again.

'How dare you!' Stripy didn't learn. He pounced again. This

time the mouse didn't dodge. Instead, it grabbed Stripy's paw and became a blur of movement.

Miiaaoow! Stripy spun away through the air and landed in a rose bush.

Milly gasped. Was that what had happened to poor Boris back in the bedroom?

'Ouch! Ouch! Ouch!' Stripy moaned as rose thorns pricked through his fur.

The mouse walked back towards Milly. It seemed completely recovered, although its back still looked matted with dried blood.

'Hello. My name's Dan.'

The mouse was holding out a paw to shake. Milly was wary of touching it again after what had happened last time – but she reached down and shook it anyway. 'I'm Milly.'

There was a rustle and a squeal as Stripy finally managed to pull himself out of the rosebush. They both looked round at him.

Stripy moaned at them. 'I'll be back!'

The cat hobbled to the garden gate and whimpered as he jumped up onto it and disappeared over the other side.

Milly turned back to the mouse. 'How did you do that?'

The mouse shrugged. 'He's just a cat, and I'm a highly trained temple mouse.'

What on earth was a temple mouse? But that question would have to wait, something more urgent was bothering Milly. 'He said he'd tell the rats,'

Dan nodded. 'And once they find out where we are, we won't be safe here.'

Milly glanced back at her house. 'Should we go back inside?'

Dan shook his head. 'I don't think that will help.'

'What else can we do?'

'There's only one way for you to be safe,' said Dan. 'You must come with me, to the temple where I live.'

'You live in a temple?' Was everything about this mouse weird?

'I can explain everything when we get there.'

Outside the fence Milly heard a voice shouting. 'They're in here!'

'We need to go,' Dan said urgently and held out his paw again.

Milly still didn't know how they'd escaped from the rats by the river – or what all this touching paws and blackness was all about. She really didn't want to do it again.

'There's no time!' Dan shouted and leapt on her back.

And everything went black again.

Milly decided she hated floating in blackness and feeling sick. She waited for the light to come back. And waited. And waited. It seemed to be going on much longer than last time. Then suddenly there was so much of light she had to squeeze her eyes shut. She felt herself falling, but unlike last time she didn't just bump down onto the ground. The falling went on and on. She opened her eyes in alarm. The first thing she saw was clouds below her, but only for a few seconds before she plummeted into them. They looked so solid she expected it to hurt but they were just made of mist. In moments she was through them and soaking wet and cold. But she didn't notice, she was too scared of what she saw next.

Mountains and valleys spread out below her, some patches darkened by the shadows of clouds, the rest brightly lit by sunlight. Streams and small lakes sparkled, and wooded hillsides looked bright and green. Milly clawed with her four paws instinctively as though she could grab hold of the air to stop herself falling.

'Oi, stop that,' squeaked a voice over the sound of the wind in Milly's ears. She remembered the mouse, it must still be on her back.

'Helppppp!' Said Milly, starting to spin slowly and watching the ground get nearer and nearer.

'Don't worry,' shouted the mouse. 'Do you see that building on the side of the big mountain? The one with the gold tower?'

Milly tried to focus but it was hard when she was panicking. Then she spotted something glinting. It could be a gold tower. But it was miles and miles away – nowhere near where they were about to be squished when they hit the ground.

'Yes,' she squeaked.

'Okay', said the mouse. 'Now think about the ground just outside the gates... not inside, that won't work. And imagine landing there nice and lightly'.

Milly did. There was nothing she would like more than to land somewhere nice and lightly. She didn't really care where it was.

'Good....' Said the mouse. 'Now, on three, let's go there.'

'What?' said Milly. 'How?'

But the mouse ignored her.

'One.... Two...,' Oh no, thought Milly, he's going to leave me behind.

'Three!'

Milly really concentrated on being safe on the ground where he said, and everything went weird and black again.

Bump! Milly felt herself land. She opened her eyes slowly.

She was outside the high walls of a building. In the nearest wall big gates stood closed and forbidding. Dan was standing next to her.

'How did we get here?' She asked him.

Dan used a mysterious voice. 'We shifted.'

'Shifted?'

Dan nodded. 'Only temple mice can do it.'

'I don't really understand what you're talking about.'

'Think of it as magic – us temple mice can just think about a place, and then we can go there.'

Dan turned and pointed at the golden gates. 'And it's

brought us all the way to the temple where I live – we'll be safe here.'

He headed towards the gates and Milly followed. She was so confused she couldn't think of any other questions to ask.

As they got there Dan started searching through the pouches in his belt.

'I've got a key somewhere,' he muttered to himself. 'Where's it gone?'

While she was waiting Milly tried pushing the gates – and to her surprise they creaked open.

'Oh!' Said Dan. 'They should be locked.'

Together they pushed the gates open further so they could squeeze through. Inside there was a huge courtyard, surrounded by high walls. As they walked into it from the shadows under the gates everything seemed quiet. They went to the middle and stood in the bright morning sunlight. Milly was glad to get her paws back on the ground – but she couldn't quite take all this in. It was like a dream – and she wasn't sure if it was a good one or a bad one.

'Where is everyone?' Wondered Dan, scratching his head and looking around.

Then the gates clanged shut behind them... and a screechy voice sang out. 'We're right here!'

The air wavered in a strange way and suddenly from all around the sides of the courtyard hostile eyes stared at Milly and Dan. More rats! And all of them holding sharp looking swords and spears.

'Oh no!' Muttered Dan.

'Ha! I told you someone had shifted outside!' A black, wiry figure said. It was bigger than the rats around it and was holding a staff up above its head in triumph.

'That's an elder's staff!' Muttered Dan.

Another black rat next to the first one looked just as pleased with itself.

'And I made everyone invisible.' That rat was holding a staff as well.

'Enough!' boomed a different voice.

'Mordred!' Gasped Dan.

Mordred? Milly saw an even bigger rat step forwards to stand next to the rats with the staffs. She was sure it was the same huge rat that had chased her by the river. His next words came as no surprise. 'Kill that cat!'

Immediately all the rats started running towards them.

What did I do? Thought Milly.

'Stop!' Squeaked Dan, jumping in front of Milly and waving his paws in a weird way. Surprisingly the rats did stop, skidding slightly and kicking up dust from the dried mud floor of the courtyard.

Dan crouched ready to fight and shouted out loud. 'If any rat wants to kill this cat, they'll have to kill me first!'

There was silence, then a hum began to grow as the rats muttered to each other. Some of them glanced across at

Mordred.

'Kill them both!' Mordred shouted and the rats leapt forward again.

'Darn it!' Said Dan and jumped onto Milly's back again. 'Run for it!'

Milly did run, but she was surrounded and whichever way she went there were more rats with swords. She ended up running round in smaller and smaller circles.

'This is no good,' Milly puffed as she ran. 'Can't you shift us away again?'

'No – not from inside the temple,' shouted Dan.

The circles were getting very small now, and there was so much dust being kicked up by lots of scrabbling paws that it was hard to see.

Suddenly a trapdoor opened in the ground right in front of Milly.

'Quick, in here!' Squeaked a new voice. Milly didn't stop to think, she just jumped through the trapdoor hole and heard it slam shut behind her.

Up ln the courtyard the rat soldiers stopped running around. Mordred came striding through the crowd.

'Are they dead?' He coughed in the settling dust. He towered over the other rats.

A small rat was pushed forward by the others.

'You tell him, Ember!' Someone hissed.

'Erm…' the small rat started nervously. 'They seem to have… gone.'

'GONE?'

'Yes. Gone. Not here.'

'I know what gone means, you silly little rat. But where could they have gone?'

Ember wished he was somewhere else, he shrugged. 'Maybe they shifted?'

Mordred pointed up at a great glowing ball that hovered in the air over the main spire of the temple. 'That's impossible, no one can shift in or out of this Temple, the orb's magic stops it.'

'I can do it,' came a sneering voice. Mordred stared at the owner of the voice. It was the black wiry rat – one of the four ninja rats that Mordred had in his army.

'Only because I gave you that elder's staff,' snapped Mordred.

Mordred was very cross. He could not believe that meddling mouse Dan had saved the cat again! He turned back to the little rat in front of him – who had been trying to shuffle away quietly.

'You!' Mordred pointed a paw at Ember. 'Stop right there!'

Then he glanced around at all the rats. 'You're all incompetent, you let a cat and a mouse slip past you broad daylight. Search the temple from top to bottom and find them!'

He pointed his huge paw at Ember. 'And if they don't find them – I will hold you responsible!'

Mordred strode away across the courtyard towards a pair of

wooden doors that led inside. They banged shut behind him and all the rats in the courtyard jumped.

'Err – all right everyone, start searching' said Ember uncertainly. '...Please...'

Underneath the courtyard in a dark tunnel Milly finally got her breath back. She was huddled down with Dan and five other mice trying not to make a sound while they heard the booming voice of the Mordred just above their heads. They could hear every word clearly.

She felt a tap on her shoulder and turned her head to look. Dan was holding one paw up to his mouth to tell her not to speak and pointing with the other paw away along the tunnel. She nodded; she thought it was a very good idea to get as far away from here as possible.

They crept along the tunnel, which was dimly lit by glowing round lights on the walls at regular intervals. Almost immediately they reached a junction where the tunnel branched into two and the mice turned right. Then only a few paces further on the tunnel branched again. This time the mice took them left. The tunnels continued to branch and turn, and Milly knew she'd never find her way back to that trapdoor on her own. And what would happen if all the lights went out? It would be pitch black down here. She hurried to keep up, as the mice weren't creeping anymore and were scurrying along quickly.

'Come along Milly!' Dan turned and waved for her to hurry.

Just then they reached a big cave, although it was more like a luxurious room. There were red and blue rugs on the floor, and flags and pictures printed on cloth hanging on the walls. There was a single light up in the rocky roof which gave a low light that made the cave seem cosy and safe. Two other tunnels led out of the cave to the left and the right through ornate stone archways.

They paused to catch their breath. Dan gasped a question.

'What's been going on here? How did those rats get into the temple?'

One of the other mice answered. He was older than Dan and wore a sword slung in a leather strap over his shoulders. 'They got in last night – took us by surprise.'

Another mouse – a bit younger – but also wearing a sword – joined in. 'We tried to fight them, but there were too many. We had to run for it and hide in the tunnels.'

The first mouse spoke again. 'Who's your cat friend?'

'This is Milly – I brought her here to help us,' Dan then waved a paw towards the group of mice. 'And Milly, these are the fight masters – they train the temple students in combat skills.'

There were five of them, all different ages, but all with scars of healed wounds and wearing swords in leather belts over their shoulders. They nodded 'hello' to Milly but seemed wary, like they didn't like having a cat in their temple any more than they did a horde of rats.

Dan asked another question. 'How did the rats get in?'

The older fight master shook his head. 'They got the gates open somehow.'

Dan gasped. 'But that's impossible, only the elders and the queen have keys,' he said, but then stopped abruptly and looked a bit sick. He started to check through the pouches of his belt again – pulling everything out and dumping it onto the floor of the cave.

'My key's gone,' he said finally.

The fight master tutted and shook his head. 'You gave the rats your key?'

'They ambushed me – I only escaped by luck. I must have dropped it.'

'Huh!' Said the another of the fight masters under his breath. 'Too young to be an elder.'

Dan nodded and stared at the ground. 'This is all my fault.'

Everyone went quiet. And in that quietness Milly heard a distant bang and clatter. They all looked towards the noise, which came from the tunnel on the right-hand side of the cave.

Dan said what they were all thinking. 'The rats have found the tunnels.'

4

Locked Up in the Dark

'This way,' hissed the older fight master, and scurried towards the archway on the left-hand side of the cave. All the other mice followed and Milly scampered after them.

'Quickly, quickly!' The mouse in the lead was running fast and Milly was finding it hard to keep up. This tunnel was winding and twisting but didn't seem to have any branches. The sound of rats behind them faded. But then suddenly the mouse in the lead stopped and they all piled into him.

'Sshh!' He whispered.

More clatters and gruff squeaks were coming from up ahead. They were trapped!

'Come on!' The mouse in front started running again in the same direction, towards the noise.

Wouldn't they just bump into a load of rats coming the other way? Milly was scared, but she kept following – what choice did she have?

At every bend in the tunnel the sound of the rats from ahead got louder. Any moment now they would run into them. Then after a particularly sharp corner the leading mouse stopped suddenly. He started scraping the wall of the tunnel, looking for something. The sound of rats from ahead was very loud now.

Then there was a grinding noise and the mouse disappeared.

'In here, quickly!' Milly heard him shout. One by one all the mice disappeared into the wall, but when Milly got there she stopped in horror. There was an open door in the wall, but the tunnel beyond looked much too small for her! Dan poked his head back through.

'Come on!' And he disappeared again.

Milly glanced up towards where the noise of the rats was coming from. She couldn't see them yet, but they had to be nearly here. She looked back at the small opening. If she tried to squeeze in and got stuck, the soldiers would pull her out and catch everyone. No. She grabbed the door and slammed it shut, then nodded to herself as she saw it merged with the rock of the wall and was impossible to see. Then she turned and ran back down the tunnel the way they had come.

'There – the cat!' Came a shout from behind her, and she heard scampering paws. She ran as fast as she could. If she could just get back to that cave and then into the maze of tunnels beyond, she might be able to hide. She was leaving the rats behind and to her relief she saw the archway of the cave entrance up ahead. In a few moments she would be safe. She dived through the archway – but then skidded to a halt.

'Ah – the cat!' Mordred was standing in the middle of the cave surrounded by soldiers.

'Meow,' said Milly and spun around to run back the way she had come, only to see the rats that had been chasing her charge into the cave.

'Grab her!' Mordred boomed.

Rats jumped on Milly from all sides. She struggled but there were too many of them, and in seconds they had her pinned to the ground. Then there was a swish of steel and she saw Mordred looming over her with his sword pointing at her heart.

'Where's that mouse that was with you?'

Milly kept quiet.

'Tell me where he went,' Mordred said quietly. 'I might even let you go.'

'You're going to kill me anyway,' she said defiantly. 'So why would I tell you?'

Mordred stared at her for a few more moments, then he raised his sword and slid it into a scabbard behind his back.

'Not yet I think,' he said. 'I want that mouse – and I think my ninja rats could find ways to help you remember where he went.... they might enjoy that.'

Milly shivered. She didn't know what ninja rats were, but they didn't sound nice.

'Take her to the dungeon!' Mordred ordered. 'And someone go and find Narvik – tell him I've got a cat for him to play with.'

Milly woke up to the smell of damp and decay. She'd just had a horrible dream. In it she'd been dragged along tunnels, bumped down steps, pulled through smelly puddles, and finally pushed into cold darkness with the sound of a door slamming shut behind her.

She looked around at the huge gloomy space surrounding her. Oh no, she thought, it wasn't a dream, it really happened. This must be the dungeon!

She pushed herself up onto her feet. She was cold and wet. She shivered.

'It's awake!' came a squeaky voice.

There was a pitter-patter of claws on stone and she found herself surrounded by a group of four mice. One of the mice, who had brown fur flecked with grey, stepped forward.

'Tell us, cat, why we should allow you to live?' He said threateningly.

Milly thought about that. 'Because you're all mice and I could just eat you?'

The mice went quiet. One of the others coughed uncomfortably. 'The cat has a good point.'

'No,' said the first mouse. 'We are the temple elders – no cat can hurt us!'

The mouse stamped his small paw on the floor of the dungeon.

'But we don't have our staffs anymore,' the other mouse

pointed out.

'We are still temple mice', the first mouse said firmly.

The mouse stood up straighter and faced Milly. She remembered how Dan had dealt with Stripy, she knew what temple mice could do. But these mice looked old and frail – except for one at the back, who looked younger, but quite small and skinny.

'Look, I'm not going to eat you!' Milly said finally. They didn't look very appetising anyway. The mice didn't look like they believed her.

'I promise,' she added. At least for now, she thought, not knowing how much hungrier she was going to get. 'I came here with a mouse called Dan – and I didn't try to eat him.'

The first mouse, who seemed to be the oldest, seemed shocked.

'But Dan is dead,' he said shaking his head.

'No, he isn't. I met him a few days ago near my house,' Milly explained. 'He saved me from a load of rats.'

The mice all looked round at the skinny one at the back.

'Hawthorn! You said Mordred had killed him!'

The skinny mouse looked at his feet uncomfortably.

'I saw blood and a broken rat sword – and he wasn't there – I just assumed...' He shrugged. 'But I'm glad he's alive!' He added.

Milly didn't think the mouse sounded very glad.

The oldest mouse turned back to Milly.

'So our new apprentice brought you here?'

Milly nodded. She assumed he meant Dan.

'Where did you last see him?' A new voice asked. A younger mouse appeared from the shadows at the back of the dungeon.

'No your majesty! Stay hidden!' The oldest mouse said in alarm. 'The cat may pounce on you!'

'I don't think she will,' said the new mouse. She looked up at Milly.

'Hello cat, my name is Queen Oleander,' she said.

'My name is Milly,' Milly replied. 'And last time I saw Dan he was still running away from the rats in the tunnels under the temple.'

From the back Milly heard the skinny mouse snort contemptuously. 'Well, we can't expect any help from him, then! The rats will soon catch him and kill him.'

Milly ignored him and looked around at the damp, smelly dungeon. 'How did you all end up in here?'

'Mordred put us in here,' said Oleander. 'I woke up last night to find my bedroom full of rats.'

'The rats took us by surprise,' the oldest mouse explained. 'Somehow they got through the gates last night'.

All the mice were shaking their heads sadly.

'The gates are enchanted,' he added. 'It's meant to be impossible to open them without a key.'

Oh! Thought Milly, immediately remembering Dan's lost key. Better not say anything.

'We were all in bed – the rats took our staffs before we could use them,' moaned one of the others.

'There should have been someone on watch!' Stated Oleander.

They all turned and glared at the skinny mouse at the back again – he looked indignant.

'I was on watch! But there were more than a hundred rats. There was nothing I could do.'

Oleander turned back to Milly. 'The rats dragged us down here and locked us in,' she glanced around. 'In our own dungeons.'

Dungeons... a queen... staffs... elders... there was so much going on here she didn't know about.

'What are elders?' She thought she'd start with that.

'We are the elders,' said the oldest mouse importantly. 'We run the temple.'

'Sorry Milly – where are our manners?' Oleander added. 'This is Ragweed, the leader of the elders, and the others are Chestnut, Damson and Acorn'. She pointed at each mouse in turn.

'And me?' The skinny mouse at the back said.

'Oh yes, and that's the other apprentice elder, Hawthorn.'

Everyone went quiet again and Milly could feel the tension in the room. Oleander was still cross. The elders glanced at each other uncomfortably. And Hawthorn just stuck his nose in the air and pretended he wasn't with them.

'Is there any way to escape from here?' Asked Milly finally, to break the silence.

'There's no way out of the dungeons,' Ragweed said. 'There's only one door, and it is unbreakable.'

One of the other mice, Milly thought his name was Damson, but had got their names a bit mixed up, shook his head. 'We'll be stuck in here forever.'

Everything really did seem quite hopeless.

But just then there was a scurrying of feet outside the dungeon and then a loud clanging as the unbreakable dungeon door was unlocked. Were the rats coming back? Maybe one of those nasty-sounding ninja rats that Mordred talked about?

'Oh no,' Milly muttered to herself.

5

Out of the Dungeon and Into the Fire

The mice scurried away into the gloomy corners of the dungeon as the door creaked open.

Six rats marched in, wearing chain mail and with sharp looking swords in their paws. Milly noticed that they hadn't closed the door behind them, and decided if she got the chance, she'd run for it and lock them all inside – especially as these rats seemed a little smaller than all the ones she'd seen so far.

'Milly the cat!' The rat at the front said in a loud voice. Milly stood up straighter. She wasn't going to hide away in some corner.

'What do you want?' She asked, looking down at the squad of rats.

'We are here,' the soldier rat lifted the visor on his helmet and winked. 'To rescue you,'

It wasn't a rat at all, it was Dan.

'Thank goodness,' she gasped. 'Why are you dressed like rat soldiers?'

'Disguise, of course!' said Dan. 'We found these clothes and

46

chain mail in one of their wagons, and guess what?'

'What?' Asked Milly.

'We've got some for you!'

One of the other mice threw a bundle to her, and she unwrapped it and saw it was a large set of chain mail. There was even a helmet.

'Wow, this really is big enough to fit me,' said Milly. She started to pull the chainmail on.

'Yes, some of those rats are huge,' said Dan.

'Dan!' Came a squeak from the back of the dungeon, and Oleander ran forward. 'It is you, isn't it?'

'Queen Oleander,' said Dan, bowing deeply. 'I'm so glad you're not hurt.'

'I'm glad you're all right too,' replied Oleander. 'I was so sad when Hawthorn came back and said Mordred had killed you.'

Oleander looked like she wanted to hug Dan. Milly wondered why she didn't – maybe it wasn't what queens did.

'Hawthorn got back?' Dan asked – he sounded surprised. 'I've been worried about him.'

'Yes,' Hawthorn appeared out of the darkness. 'The rats attacked me too, but I managed to get away.'

'Really?' Dan looked shocked. 'You'll have to tell me how you managed that sometime.'

Hawthorn didn't reply.

'It fits!' Shouted Milly, as she pulled on a helmet that covered her ears.

'Very good!' Said Dan when he saw her. 'With that grey fur and your catty head and ears covered, you look like a very big fluffy rat.'

Great – thought Milly – disguised as a rat. She hoped that Stripy back at home never got to hear about this.

'Now we have to go!' Said Dan, pulling Milly by the paw. 'While we still can.'

Hawthorn's voice cut in. 'Is this a good idea? Wouldn't we be safer staying here?'

Ragweed nodded. 'The senior apprentice has a point – maybe that would be safer.'

Oleander glared at them both. 'We won't get our temple back locked in a dungeon.'

She stalked away towards the open dungeon door and Milly, Dan and fight masters rushed after her. Behind them the elders looked at each other, then reluctantly followed as well.

Outside there was a long, stony passageway. They stepped through some stinky puddles that Milly remembered from her dream – that had turned out to be real – and headed towards a stone archway at the far end. But as they got close to it there was a sudden sound of marching feet coming the other way. Before they could do anything a squad of soldier rats appeared. The rats stopped when they saw Milly and the mice.

'Hold it right there,' the rat at the front spat. 'No one is meant to be down here.'

'You're right – no-one is – so what are you doing here?' said

Dan.

That flustered the rat. 'I've got orders from Mordred – to get the cat and take it to the questioning room.'

Dan smiled. 'I only had orders to get the mice. You can have the cat, it's still back in the dungeon.'

Milly wondered what he was talking about, but then remembered she was disguised as a rat. She growled. She was suddenly fed up with being dragged here and there, being dressed up as a rat, and with everyone wanting to kill her.

The rat at the front heard the growl and glanced at her. He looked shocked and stepped backwards.

'Narvik! I'm sorry, I didn't know you were here.' The rat seemed to think Milly was someone else and was terrified.

Dan elbowed Milly and beckoned her to lean down so he could whisper in her ear. 'He thinks you're one of the ninja rats.'

Milly thought for a moment, then...

'Out of my way!' She commanded, making her voice deep.

The rats immediately stepped to one side to let them go by, bowing and keeping their eyes on the ground. Milly couldn't resist giving the lead rat a bat with her paw as she passed him, and he went flying backwards into the wall.

They walked out through the archway and on into a large hallway, while behind them there were clatters as the rats started moving again towards the dungeon. Surely it would only be moments before they discovered no one was there and came running back?

Dan rushed them all up a wide staircase and then away along a corridor at the top. There were doors at regular intervals on both sides. Milly thought they might lead to classrooms, or bedrooms, or even offices. She didn't know which, she just hoped no one came out of any of them.

As they hurried along Milly heard Oleander gasp a question to Dan. 'What do we do now? Those rats will see the dungeon is empty in no time, and then they'll come after us'.

Hawthorn gasped from the back. 'We should have stayed in the dungeon, we were safe there!'

One of the others moaned. 'They'll kill us all now.'

'Just follow me,' Dan called back in exasperation. 'I know a way out – a secret passage.'

Ragweed, the leader of the elders, stopped suddenly with a shocked look on his face. 'That's just a myth! There's no secret passage out of the temple.'

That made everyone else stop and look back at him.

Dan whispered loudly in response. 'There is a passage, one of my friends found it when we were students – we used it as a shortcut to the town.'

Ragweed was outraged. 'And you never told anyone?'

Oleander stepped between Dan and Ragweed.

'There's no time for this!' She announced, and then turned to Dan. 'Lead us to your passage, Dan – we have to get out of here now!'

Dan nodded and set off again down the corridor. Oleander

followed him and everyone else had no choice but to do the same. At the end of the corridor there was another one leading left and right. Dan went left. There were more doors in each wall, and this time there were side corridors as well, all of them leading off into darkness. Dan ignored all of them until finally he paused, looked around, then turned right down one that was pitch black.

'I think it's this way,' he muttered to himself, and they all groped along the new corridor slowly.

Hawthorn tutted from the back. 'You "think"?'

'Here!' Dan whispered.

Milly heard a click and then a scraping sound, and a square of light opened in the left-hand wall. Dan led them through the opening. 'Come on! Whoever's last shut the door!'

The other side of the opening was a passageway with rough stone walls. It was lit by an orange glow that was flickering slightly. It was quite narrow, and they all went in single file. Hawthorn came through the door last and hesitated before shutting it. He glanced at the others – who were hurrying away down the dimly lit passageway – then took his paw away from the door, leaving it open, before scampering after them.

Up at the front Milly gasped a question to Dan. 'Where's the light coming from?'

'I don't know,' Dan replied. 'It always used to be dark.'

The light became brighter as they went, and they finally reached another archway. The stones of the archway had carvings of mice all over them, and when Milly looked closer it seemed like the carved mice were covered in fire.

'I've got a nasty feeling,' said Dan.

Beyond the archway the passage stopped and there was a wide ledge. The ledge looked out into a large cavern. From there they could see where the light was coming from.

Along the bottom of the cavern flowed a river of bubbling lava!

6

Magic Steppingstones

'So how do we get past that lava?' Asked Milly. She didn't want to end up looking like one of the carvings of the mice covered in flames. Dan looked as shocked as everyone else.

'I've never seen lava here before,' he said.

'So you've led us into another trap, then?' Hawthorn said nastily.

Dan threw him a glance. To Milly it looked as though Dan wanted to say something – but he paused and kept quiet instead.

'Is there any way across?' Asked Oleander.

'Yes,' said Dan.

He went to the back of the ledge and bent down – then came back to the front edge with something in his paw. He threw a spray of dust out over the lava.

To Milly's surprise, some of the dust landed on flat round pieces of stone that seemed to hover in mid-air.

'They're invisible unless you throw dust on them,' Dan explained. 'We never knew what they were for, but I suppose this is why they're here, so you can get to the other side when there's no other way.'

Milly looked at the stones warily. 'But they don't go all the way across.'

'They do,' replied Dan. 'But you need to take more dust as you go and keep throwing it so you can see them.'

It looked very scary to Milly. But the stones weren't far apart and they should be easy to jump between, at least for her.

'Well, there's no point standing here thinking about it,' said Oleander, and she went to the back of the ledge to where Dan had got the dust and came back with two paws full.

'Wait – let me go first!' Said Dan. 'I know where...'

But Oleander had already jumped to the first stone.

'Queens!' Dan muttered under his breath. 'They just do what they want!'

He ran to to get more dust and then scampered back to take a flying leap onto the first stone himself. By that time Oleander was three stones ahead and throwing more dust out in front of her.

Milly watched as new stones appeared. They weren't in a straight line across the cavern – each one seemed to be in a random direction from the last.

Better get started, she thought. But as she looked down to jump to the first stone, she found that it had disappeared! For the first time she noticed a slight breeze ruffling her fur – it must be blowing the dust off!

Milly ran to the back of the ledge and found the pile of dust the mice had been using. She grabbed two pawfuls, then came back and threw dust like she'd seen Dan do.

The first stones appeared again – and she started jumping while she could still see them.

She stared at each stone and jumped carefully, trying not to think about the lava below. It was hard though, because the lava was giving off tremendous heat and making her feel dizzy. Ahead of her she could see that Oleander and Dan had got to about the middle but seemed to be stuck. She quickly caught up and paused on the stone behind them.

'What's wrong?' She called to them.

'We've run out of dust!' Oleander said back.

'This wind wasn't here before – it's blowing the dust around too much,' added Dan.

Milly threw some dust past Dan and Oleander's stone.

'You still have some left!' Exclaimed Oleander. 'I thought we were stuck.'

Milly's dust had landed on a bigger stone at the centre of the cavern. Oleander immediately jumped onto it, followed by Dan. Milly jumped onto the stone they had just left and, realising the bigger stone had enough room for all of them, jumped across to that too.

She joined the mice at the far edge of the big stone. There were no further stones to be seen.

'I hope you've got some more dust, Milly,' said Dan

anxiously.

Milly showed him the whole pawful she had left.

'You have bigger paws than us,' said Oleander.

Milly shared some dust with both of them.

'Let me go first this time,' Dan said.

He threw some of his dust and then started jumping. Oleander went next, and then Milly. They went as fast as they could, knowing now that the dust would blow away quickly.

Milly concentrated.

Jump... skid, stop. Look at the next stone. Jump... skid, stop. Look at the next stone. Jump... skid, stop.

She went on for four, five, six stones; trying to ignore the lava, and throwing dust whenever it seemed the stone ahead was getting faint.

Seven, eight, nine stones...

Then there was a frightened squeak ahead of her.

Milly looked up and saw Dan had reached the other side – but was looking back in horror.

Between them Oleander had reached the last stone from the end... but she must have slipped because she'd lost her balance and was about to fall off.

Milly could see the outline of four more stones between her and the queen – but they were very faint. She didn't have time to throw any more dust, so she just jumped and hoped, without pausing between each stone.

Jump... jump... jump... jump...

Oleander finally lost her balance completely as Milly was jumping to the stone she was on. She fell – paws flailing desperately to try to save herself.

Milly lunged out one paw as she landed on Oleander's stone. Jump...

Milly's last jump took her onto the ledge on the far side of the cavern, knocking over Dan as she landed.

Dan got up quickly. 'Milly – you saved her!'

Dangling from Milly's paw – with one long cat claw hooked through the tunic she was wearing – Oleander looked terrified. Milly put her down. Both mice watched with open mouths as Milly's claw disappeared again into her paw.

'How did you manage to do that?' Asked Dan in an amazed voice.

'Oh – I'm used to catching mice.'

Milly smiled. The mice tried to smile back – but didn't quite manage it.

Milly turned back to look behind them across the cavern.

'Oh dear,' she said.

None of the other mice had even started coming across. The elders were huddled in a frightened group, and the fight masters seemed unwilling to leave them.

'I suppose it's best they didn't try,' said Dan. 'One of them would've fallen in.'

Just then there were shouts and a clatter of armour as rat soldiers burst out of the passageway behind the other mice.

They were running so fast that two of them nearly fell into the lava. Milly, Dan and Oleander ducked away into the tunnel on their side of the cavern before the soldiers saw them.

'Where are the others?' Milly heard a rat Sergeant shout.

She, Dan and Oleander were peeping around the edge of the passageway that led away from the cavern. On the other side of the lava the five fight masters had jumped in front of the elders and had their swords out ready to fight.

None of them answered the rat sergeant.

'Not talking, eh? Throw one of them into the lava!' The rat ordered.

Oh no, thought Milly, this was going to be bad.

She was just about to jump out and shout to show the rats where they were when Ragweed stepped forward between the fight masters and spoke sternly to the soldiers.

'Don't you dare! You'll regret it if you harm any of us.'

'And who are you to give me orders?' The rat Sergeant glared at Ragweed.

'I am the leader of the elders,' he said.

'The leader, eh?' said the rat. 'Well, if you're the leader, you can tell these mice you've got with you to throw down their weapons.'

'If I do, will you promise not to harm us?' Asked Ragweed.

The Sergeant shrugged then nodded.

Ragweed turned to the fight masters. 'Throw down your swords!'

Milly saw them hesitate. Then Ragweed shouted. 'That's an order!'

One by one they dropped their swords onto the ground and the rats gathered them up.

'Now, where did we get to?' Said the Sergeant, scratching his head. 'Oh yes – throw one of them into the lava!'

Ragweed looked stunned. 'What? You promised!'

The rat sergeant smiled. 'Never trust a rat.'

The rats moved towards the mice. The mice stepped backwards – glancing behind them at the drop into the lava. Then Hawthorn shouted out. 'They went across to the other side!'

'Across that lava?' The Sergeant asked in disbelief.

Hawthorn nodded.

All the rats looked across the cavern – some of their mouths dropped open.

'How?' The Sergeant asked.

'There are invisible stepping stones,' Hawthorn squeaked. Milly was shocked. Why was he telling them everything?

The Sergeant scratched his head. 'If they're invisible – how did they know where to jump?'

'Dust!' Hawthorn exclaimed, then stuttered into silence as he realised all the other mice were glaring at him.

'Aha!' The Sergeant smiled and looked around, then walked

to the back of the cavern and grabbed a pawful of dust.

Watching from the other side, Oleander nudged Dan. 'Do you think we should get away from here?'

'Not yet,' said Dan. 'Let's see what happens.'

The Sergeant threw his pawful of dust out over the lava and the first few stones came into view again.

'All right – who's first?' He shouted.

None of the rats said anything.

'Ember?' The Sergeant shouted.

A small rat was pushed forwards.

'Ah there you are – nice easy job for you... off you go then,' the Sergeant said.

'Err – I'd rather not.'

'Good rat! Always ready to let someone else have all the fun! But no, it's your turn this time!'

The small rat looked at the stones. He decided it didn't actually look too hard to jump between them – but the lava was very scary. Then he felt a shove in his back and had no choice but to jump to the first stone with a squeak.

'Well done, Ember, keep going,' the Sergeant looked back at the rest of the rats. 'All right, Ember can do it, so who's next?'

All the rats stared at the floor.

'I said who's next?'

One rat put his paw up.

'Well done – off you go!'

'Actually, I wasn't volunteering, I just wanted to tell you that

Ember is waving at you,' said the rat.

The sergeant turned back to look at Ember. He'd reached the fourth stone and stopped. 'What are you doing?'

'I can't see the next one.'

'Then throw some more dust.'

'I haven't got any.'

The Sergeant sighed and shook his head. 'Someone get some dust and take it out to him.'

All the rats stared at the ground again.

'Someone? Anyone?'

They all looked scared, and a few of them were glancing at each other sideways. The sergeant could guess what they were thinking – that maybe they should just throw their sergeant into the lava rather than be forced to try the stones.

The sergeant grunted... no point in pushing his luck. 'All right then. I think we're all agreed it's impossible to get across, let's just take this lot back to the dungeon.'

The rats looked relieved and started to herd the mice back into the passageway they had come from. Then a plaintive voice made the Sergeant look back as he started to follow them away.

'Er – excuse me, sir.'

Ember was still out over the lava and looking frantically around him. All of the stones had disappeared now – even the one he was standing on. The Sergeant sighed in exasperation. 'Yes?'

'How do I get back?'

The Sergeant shrugged and turned away again, calling back over his shoulder as he walked away.

'I don't know. You got yourself into this, Ember – you get yourself out.'

From across the other side of the lava Milly watched as the soldiers and the mice left. At least no one had got hurt, she thought. One rat was still in the cavern, stuck on the stones and looking frantically around him. He didn't seem to know how to get back to the other side.

'Come on Milly, we have to go,' Dan tugged her paw. She stopped watching the rat and turned to follow him and Oleander along the passageway that led away from the lava cavern.

'Will there be any more lava?' She asked.

'I hope not,' said Dan.

Oleander turned to Dan. 'I'm worried about that lava, do you know why it's there?'

'Yes,' Dan replied. 'I think the legend of the mountain is coming true.'

Oleander gasped.

'What legend?' Milly asked.

'What are we going to do?' Oleander whispered.

'Either run away – or try to stop it,' Dan replied grimly.

'What legend?' Milly asked.

'We can't run away – we have to save the temple!'

'I agree – we should do that, if we can,' said Dan.

'What legend?' Milly asked.

'But how can we stop it?' Asked Oleander.

'The legend shows only one way,' answered Dan.

'What legend?' Milly asked.

They both stopped and turned to look at her.

'The cat!' said Oleander in wonder.

'Yes, I think Milly is the cat,' said Dan.

Milly looked at them suspiciously. 'What legend?' She asked. 'And what do you mean – I'm the cat?'

'The legend of the mountain is carved into the walls of our great hall,' explained Oleander. 'It's one of my favourites'.

She shivered. 'Or at least it used to be. The first pictures show lava streams like we just crossed.'

'Then the next ones show the ground shaking,' said Dan.

'Then clouds of smoke in the sky,' said Oleander.

'Then a great eruption destroying everything,' they both said together.

'Meow,' said Milly. 'I think I want to go home.'

The mice looked at her.

'But you're the cat,' said Oleander. 'We need your help.'

'Oh,' said Milly. 'I'm the cat.'

They both nodded.

'Like – THE cat, right?'

They nodded again.

'I have no idea what you're talking about,' she said.

Dan paused, about to go on explaining, then he seemed to change his mind. 'We'll tell you everything, Milly – but not here – we need to get to safety first. We may not be the only ones who know about this secret passage.'

7

The Legend of the Cat

Hawthorn stumbled as he was pushed through a set of high double doors by two rats. He knew where he was – the chamber of the elders. And inside Mordred was waiting for him.

'Leave us!' Mordred shouted at the rats, and they ran out quickly.

'And close the doors after you!' One of them scampered back and pulled the doors closed.

Hawthorn straightened his robes. 'It's about time!' He complained. 'That dungeon was very smelly.'

'I'm sorry,' said Mordred, not looking sorry at all. 'But you didn't want everyone knowing you were a traitor.'

As the big rat spoke a metal circle embedded in the floor flashed colours in time with his words. When he said 'traitor' a red line shot around the whole thing.

'Why are you standing in the circle?' Asked Hawthorn.

The metal circle was about five paces across and took up most of the chamber.

Mordred looked down at it. 'I like it.'

More colours chased themselves around the circle.

'But the elders use the circle to send out messages. Someone might be able to hear everything you say.'

'Really? So why did the Weasel tell me that *all* of the elders had to be present to use it to send a message.'

What a smug rat! Of course, he was right, but the circle still made Hawthorn nervous. There was no way he was going to stand inside it. He gave an annoyed shrug and changed the subject. 'What are you and your rats doing here in the temple anyway? Weren't you meant to wait down by the bridge?'

'That was the original plan. But something went wrong,' Mordred said. 'Something called Dan. He is a very troublesome mouse.'

Colours continued to flash around the circle as he spoke – making Hawthorn cringe.

'Yes, he is – he's been trying to get me killed all day!' Hawthorn complained. 'I thought you'd dealt with him at the Weasel's burrow.'

'So did I – but he must be a good swimmer – because he somehow survived falling in the river and then came and snatched the cat before we could kill it.'

'Yes – I've seen the cat too,' Hawthorn said. 'Big, nasty, fluffy thing.'

'Indeed. Anyway, I thought to myself, if Dan has the cat, what will he do with it?'

Mordred glanced around the walls. 'And I decided he would

have to come here, to your precious temple. After all, where else could he somehow use a cat to stop the eruption? So, I decided to come here too – so I could catch them both.'

Hawthorn smiled nastily. 'And yet they seem to have got away from you again. The Weasel will be cross about all these mistakes.'

Mordred gave Hawthorn a long stare – then spoke again at last. 'Only if someone tells him.'

Mordred walked out of the circle at last and Hawthorn sighed with relief. The big rat went over to a table at the end of the room and picked something up. Hawthorn's eyes widened when he saw what it was. It was a staff. Ragweed's staff, the staff of conquest. Mordred held it by one end and let it swing back and forth in his paw. Hawthorn wondered if he had any idea how powerful it was. He made his way carefully around the outside of the circle and over to the table.

'You should be careful – that's an elder's staff.'

Mordred smiled. 'I know. Do you want it?'

'Yes!' Hawthorn gasped.

Apprentices didn't have staffs of their own, but they did get to practice with them. Hawthorn knew how to use it.

Mordred was smiling. 'I'd give it to you if I could trust you... trust you not to, say, go telling tales to the weasel.'

Hawthorn nodded quickly. 'I won't.'

Mordred pretended to think about it, then slowly held the staff out to Hawthorn. The mouse snatched it eagerly and studied it. He was right, it was the staff of conquest! Probably the most powerful of all the staffs. But what had Mordred done with the others?

'Are the other staffs safe?'

Mordred smirked. 'Maybe... I've given them to the ninja rats.'

Those disgusting creatures that worked for Mordred? They wouldn't know how to use the staffs properly but... he shivered... the staffs would still make them very dangerous. 'I'm not sure the Weasel will be happy with that.'

'Didn't we just agree no one would be telling tales to the weasel?' Said Mordred. 'And anyway, he'll be happy just so long as this temple gets destroyed.'

Hawthorn shrugged. He thought Mordred had been lucky to get away with attacking the temple.

'What you did was dangerous,' he said. 'If the elders hadn't been taken by surprise it would be you and your rats locked up in the dungeons now.'

'Rubbish,' scoffed Mordred. 'A bunch of gossiping old mice? Now if they were all like that Dan, then I might start to worry.'

'The elders were powerful once,' muttered Hawthorn.

'Yes – they were – but that time is past. Now they are old and weak and all you high-and-mighty temple mice just wander round the world enjoying yourselves,' Mordred sneered. 'It's time for the rats to take over.'

So that's what the weasel promised you, thought Hawthorn,

as he cradled the staff in his paws and stared at it. But that wasn't the real plan. The real plan was for the mice to have a new king. There hadn't been one for hundreds of years, not since the last king disappeared. But now Hawthorn would become the new king, once this temple was buried in lava and the weasel had taken over Mouse City. King Hawthorn would make the mice great again!

'Are you daydreaming about how great the new rat empire will be?' Mordred asked sarcastically.

Hawthorn jumped – had Mordred guessed what he was thinking? No... the big rat didn't even know how powerful a gift this staff was. Now it was in his possession, Hawthorn didn't really need to be afraid of the rat anymore, in fact it should be the other way round.

'No – I'm not actually,' he said. 'Anyway, what do you plan to do next?'

'Nothing,' said Mordred. 'Ideally I wanted to kill Dan and that cat – but now they've escaped again I just want to keep them out of the temple so they can't interfere.'

Hawthorn thought about the legend. He'd read all the books in the library that said anything about it – that's where he'd found the spell that he and the weasel had used to start the eruption. But the cat was a mystery. It wasn't mentioned in any of the books – it was only shown in one carving on the wall of the great hall. He had no idea how the cat might be used to stop the eruption – and he was sure Dan didn't know either. Maybe

Mordred was right... and all they had to do was keep Dan and his cat out of the temple.

While he was thinking these thoughts Mordred had walked back towards the circle. But he stopped at its edge this time, much to Hawthorn's relief.

'Can this circle really send out a message to every temple mouse in the world?' He asked.

'With enough elders standing in it, yes,' confirmed Hawthorn. He'd seen it used once himself, when he was a new apprentice – to organise the search for the previous queen, Oleander's mother, after she went missing.

'Maybe we should try smashing it?' Pondered Mordred.

'I'd be careful,' said Hawthorn. 'There's a lot of magical power locked up in it.'

'I suppose it will be destroyed anyway by the mountain,' said Mordred. 'And once it's gone the elders will have no way to send a message – no way to pull their army together... and with no mouse army, nothing will stand in my way!'

'Our way,' reminded Hawthorn.

'Yes, of course,' Mordred agreed. 'Our way.'

It took Milly, Dan and Oleander another hour to reach the end of the tunnel. When they got there they slowed down, suddenly wary of what might be waiting for them outside.

Dan peeked out, and Milly and Oleander held their breath

70

behind him.

'All clear,' he whispered.

The tunnel came out in a small cave in the hillside below the temple. Outside the cave a yellow moon cast dim light over the landscape – and further down the hill a mass of lights twinkled.

'What's that?' Asked Milly.

'The town,' replied Dan. 'That's where we're going.'

Milly sighed. No one had mentioned any town. She felt like she was just being dragged from one place to another with no idea of where she was or what was happening. But there was no time to ask any questions now. Dan and Oleander had already scurried ahead down a steep path, and all she could do was follow on behind.

The path wound back and forth down the hillside, hardly visible in the faint moonlight, and small rocks and stones skittered away under Milly's paws as she tried to keep up.

Finally, the path started to level off, and soon afterwards it joined a wider mud road that led towards the town. This was much easier to walk on and Milly found she was able to look up at the town they were approaching.

'Wow! It has walls and gates, like a castle,' she exclaimed.

'Yes, it is like a castle,' agreed Dan. 'But the gates look like they're open.'

'I hope the rats aren't here as well,' breathed Oleander.

'Me too,' said Dan. 'Anyway, we'll soon find out.'

They reached the gates and started to walk through.

'Stop right there!' A rough voice shouted.

Milly peered towards where the voice came from. A large shape lumbered out from a doorway in the left-hand gate tower.

'Dan,' the voice rumbled. 'Good to see you.'

'Humble, you're working nights now?' Dan replied with a laugh, and Milly could hear from the tone of his voice that everything was going to be okay.

'Yes – what with all the rumbling in the ground and such – I wanted to keep an eye on things myself tonight.'

Now he was closer Milly could see the guard was a large mouse, not a rat. The guard peered at Milly suspiciously, and she had to hold herself back from hissing at him.

'See you've got a cat with you – fat one by the looks of it.'

Fat? Milly let the hiss out and the guard stepped back.

'Steady now – no offence meant,' he said.

'She's a good friend,' said Oleander.

The mouse guard bowed low when he heard her voice. 'And Queen Oleander, forgive me. I didn't see you there in the dark. If this cat's a friend of yours she's a friend of mine. So long as she doesn't try to eat me.'

Milly screwed up her nose. 'You're too smelly to eat.'

Humble laughed. 'Right you are, I am smelly, and with all the cats in the town these days it's the best way to be – none of them want to come near me.'

Dan stepped closer to Humble to talk in a low voice. 'There's trouble at the temple.'

Humble groaned. 'What's happened?'

'Mordred and about a hundred of his rats – they got in when no one was looking – and I expect the rest of his army will be lurking about somewhere,' Dan replied.

Humble shook his head. 'I've always said there should be a full squad of mouse guards up there.'

He glanced through the gates – looking worriedly into the darkness beyond. It seemed odd to Milly that he was looking down the hill, and not up towards the temple. His next words made no sense to her.

'There's been no report from the guards on the bridge all day – I'd bet my pension there's more rats down there.'

What bridge? No-one had mentioned any bridge.

Humble shook himself and turned back to them. 'I'll call out the rest of the guards... and I'll get these gates closed up tight.'

The cat and the two mice watched him as he lumbered back to the gate tower. Despite his size he moved quickly.

'Good mouse, Humble,' murmured Dan, nodding to himself. They carried on walking into the town, and before they were out of sight of the gates, they heard them squeal as they were pulled shut and barred from the inside.

'What did he mean about not having mouse guards up at the temple?' Asked Milly. She was quite tired and not sure she wanted to think any more tonight – but it had been bothering her that there seemed to be so few mice in the temple.

'Humble's the captain of the guards in the town,' explained

Dan. 'They have their barracks down here – and their job is to protect the town and the temple'.

'So there's no guards in the temple itself?'

'No, just the elders who teach the students magic, and the fight masters who teach them how to fight.'

Milly heard Oleander sigh to herself in the darkness. 'And me of course – I've lived there too for the last couple of years.'

Oleander sounded sad as she said that – Milly wondered why.

'So where do the students live?' Milly asked.

'Here in the town,' said Dan. 'There's a dormitory near the guardhouse – and some live with mouse families too.'

They walked up the main street between darkened shops and lit-up eating houses and taverns.

Milly yawned.

'I'm tired,' she said. 'And hungry.'

Dan brought them to a stop outside a tavern.

'This is a good place – I know the owner and we'll all be welcome,' he said.

'A word of warning Milly,' said Oleander. 'I know you are a good cat, but just in case you're tempted, don't eat any mice in this town.'

'Why not?' Asked Milly.

'Well, this tavern was named after the last cat who ate a mouse here'.

Milly looked up at the sign on the wall of the tavern. It was called 'The Hanging Cat'.

That night Milly at last had something to eat – dried fish and water. The mice had large chunks of cheese. After that they went upstairs to a guest room where Milly curled up and was fast asleep within seconds. She dreamed of being back home, where there were no soldiers or magic mice or exploding mountains.

The next morning Milly woke up and stretched before opening her eyes. For a moment she thought she was sleeping on her favourite cushion at home. Then she opened her eyes and remembered where she really was. In a small room in a tavern on the slopes of a weird mountain. There was no furniture in the room, just six sacks stuffed with something prickly. Only three were being used, her own and the ones Dan and Oleander were laying on. The two mice were still asleep and seeing them made Milly's stomach rumble. She instantly felt guilty about having hungry thoughts, and it made her think about the sign outside the tavern with the picture of the cat hanging up by its feet. She wondered if they really did that to cats who ate mice here.

Dan stirred and sat up and looked at Milly suspiciously.

Milly smiled sweetly. 'Good morning.'

Dan nodded and yawned, then got up and woke Oleander.

They all went downstairs to have breakfast – more dried fish and water for Milly – she wondered if cats ever got to eat anything else around here.

Dan and Oleander were very quiet. They only nibbled at their cheese and didn't seem hungry.

'What's wrong?' Asked Milly.

'We need to decide what to do next,' Dan said.

Milly thought for a bit. 'Shouldn't we warn everyone in the town, so they can leave before the mountain blows up?'

Dan shook his head. 'Humble sent some mice down to the bridge last night – and it's like we thought, swarming with rat soldiers.'

Milly realised she'd never got the chance to ask about the bridge everyone kept talking about. 'What is the bridge?'

Oleander answered. 'The Temple and this town are on the high slopes of a mountain. It's very steep and the only easy way on or off the mountain is to use a long bridge that crosses the valley.'

'Oh,' said Milly. She looked around at the other tables – they were full of cats and mice. If they couldn't use the bridge to get out, would they all be killed?

'Couldn't everyone shift away?' Milly tried.

'The guards could do that because they're temple mice – but normal mice can't shift,' said Oleander.

'You shifted me here,' said Milly. 'Couldn't you and the guards do the same and shift everyone else away?'

'Shifting with someone else is hard,' said Dan. 'It would take us months to get everyone out the town to safety.'

'Oh.'

They all went quiet again and the mice went on nibbling at their breakfast.

Milly thought of something else. 'Didn't you say yesterday that we could try to stop the mountain from blowing up?'

Dan looked at her. 'Is that what you really want to do?'

'No – I actually want to go home,' said Milly. 'But then those rats might come back and try to kill me again... so it looks like trying to stop the mountain is my only option.'

Oleander looked at her sympathetically.

'Thank you, Milly,' she said, then she turned to Dan.

'I still don't understand exactly how all this happened,' she said. 'How did you find out about Milly and the mountain and everything?'

'It's a long story,' said Dan. 'But we seem to have time for it.'

He told them both about his trip to the Weasel's burrow with Hawthorn.

Oleander grabbed his paw when he said he'd been washed away in the river. 'Thank goodness you weren't drowned.'

Dan looked surprised that the queen was holding his paw – but he kept on talking. He told them how he eventually managed to drag himself out of the water when the river emptied out into a big lake downstream. And how once he'd recovered from being half-drowned, he'd decided Hawthorn would never get past the rats outside the weasel's burrow, and it was up to him to go and get the cat.

'So that's me right – the cat?' Asked Milly.

Dan nodded.

'And what do you mean exactly by calling me 'the cat'?'

Oleander answered her question. 'Although the carving of the legend shows the mountain blowing up and everything being destroyed, there is a part that shows another possible ending.'

She paused, and Milly nodded for her to go on.

'That other ending shows the orb over the temple shining brightly, and the mountain calming back down – and on the orb there is a face – the face of a cat.'

'And you think that's me?' Asked Milly. 'Because I don't know anything about orbs or magic or stopping mountains exploding.'

'We hope it's you,' said Dan.

'*Hope* it's me?' Spluttered Milly.

'Well, I shifted to the exact place the weasel put in my head – and you were there.'

'But you don't actually know?'

Dan shrugged and Milly glared at him.

Oleander cut into the tense silence. 'So how did you both end up here?'

Dan and Milly took turns in telling Oleander about how Dan had saved her from the rats, and how they'd got to the temple – right up to when Milly had been thrown in the dungeons.

'So, assuming Milly is the cat in the legend – how does she save the temple?' Asked Oleander.

Dan smiled. 'She uses the orb.'

'But how does she do that? It's hovering high up in the sky over the temple.' Asked Oleander.

'Actually, no.'

Dan pulled a piece of paper out from a pouch in his belt. It had a ragged, torn edge. 'I got this from the temple library...'

Before he could go on Oleander drew in a shocked breath and let go of his paw. 'You tore a page out of one of the books?'

Dan looked embarrassed. 'I needed it – it's from one of the big old books – it was much too heavy to carry the whole thing.' He sounded like he was trying to convince himself.

Oleander gave him a disapproving glare.

'Look,' Dan smoothed the page out on the table. 'This talks about the true orb, and says it's hidden in the middle of the mountain.'

Despite herself, Oleander looked interested.

'It says the orb over the spire is just an image – a reflection of the power of the true orb inside the mountain.'

'I never knew that,' Oleander said. 'Does that page say how to get to it?'

Dan nodded.

'It says there's a pathway through the mountain that leads to it.'

'Let me look!' Oleander reached over, slid the page towards

her and started reading.

'Hmmm...' she said as she read.

'Oh!' She gasped, as she read one bit.

She glanced up at Dan. 'Have you read all of this?'

Dan nodded.

Oleander went back to reading.

'That's weird!' She gasped as she got to the end of the page. She turned the page over and tutted.

'Isn't there any more?' She asked.

'No – at least I don't think so – maybe I should have torn out more pages.'

'It's missing what to do when you find the orb.'

'I know – but at least it explains how to get to it.'

Milly was looking from one to the other as they spoke – it was like they'd forgotten she was there.

'So – are you two saying we have to find some sort of path through the mountain to get to this orb thing – and then I'm supposed to use to save everyone?' Milly asked.

They both nodded.

She looked around the room. Up until now she'd just been following everyone around trying not to get killed... but now suddenly it was up to her to save the lives of everyone on this mountain?

Dan and Oleander seemed to have regained their appetites and were chomping through the rest of their cheese. But Milly wasn't hungry anymore. She pushed her plate away. What had she got herself into now?

'I'm glad you made it back across that lava all right, Ember,' the rat sergeant said cheerfully as he led the smaller rat along a passageway. Ember had never been into the main part of mouse temple before and looked around in amazement. It seemed they had gone up so many flights of steps that they must be near the very top.

'Got a nice easy job for you,' the sergeant went on as he walked.

They finally approached two high double doors that were closed. The sergeant turned to Ember and handed him a metal pickaxe with a wooden handle. It was big and heavy.

The sergeant then pushed the double doors open and went through.

Ember followed and found himself in an amazing room. But he didn't have much time to stare because Mordred himself was waiting there.

'About time!' snapped Mordred.

Lights in the floor chased themselves in a circle around Mordred as he spoke – it was fascinating.

'Don't I know you?' Mordred boomed at Ember. More lights flickered in a circle around the floor.

Ember stood at attention and stared at a point behind Mordred's left shoulder. 'I don't think so, sir.'

'Hmmm,' said Mordred, then turned his attention to the sergeant. 'Well – get on with it – report back to me with the results.'

Mordred left the room quickly and Ember sighed in relief.

'All right lad,' said the sergeant. 'Bit of fun for you here.'

He pointed at the floor.

Ember saw a metal circle embedded in the flagstones. It was big – about ten paces across. He realised that the lights he had seen when Mordred spoke earlier had been flickering around this circle.

'You just need to dig up this circle thing – get it out of the flagstones and break it up,' said the sergeant. 'Easy bit of work for a strong rat like yourself.'

Ember sighed. It was typical for him to get this sort of hard, boring job. He sighed and raised the pickaxe over his head, aiming to take a first swing to see how tough the flagstones were.

'Easy, easy,' the sergeant said, putting a paw up on the pickaxe to stop it. 'I'll just pop outside... make sure all your banging doesn't disturb anyone.'

Ember watched as his sergeant left the room and closed the double doors behind him. Then he raised the pickaxe over his head again. Very peculiar behaviour, he thought, as he swung the pickaxe down at the metal circle.

The sergeant waited in the passageway outside the chamber of the elders – with his paws over his ears.

Boom!

The high double doors were blown off their hinges and hit the other side of the passageway, then clattered to the floor. Purple smoke billowed out of the room.

The sergeant waited a few moments while the smoke cleared, then carefully peeped around the edge of the shattered doorway. The circle in the floor was still there and looked undamaged. But there was no sign of Ember anywhere. The Sergeant shrugged, then hurried away to report to Mordred.

8

Way of the Three Blind Mice

Milly stood with Dan and Oleander high on the walls of the town. Humble was next to them; he'd just finished his night duty and was about to head off for bed. Up above them thick, black smoke was drifting out of the top of the mountain.

'That smoke wasn't there yesterday,' said Humble, twitching his whiskers worriedly.

Milly squinted as rays of light from the morning sun shafted through the smoke. It would have been quite beautiful if it didn't seem so deadly.

'We found a lava flow inside the mountain yesterday,' Dan told Humble.

Humble sighed. 'Do you think the legend's coming true? Is the mountain going to blow up?'

'I think so.'

'But we won't be able to get everyone out – not with those rats on the bridge,' worried Humble.

'We're going to try to stop it,' said Oleander.

'Stop it – how?'

Dan pointed with one paw in a different direction.

'By using the orb.'

Milly's gaze followed where he pointed and she saw a round thing hovering over the temple, directly above a gold central tower that speared up into the sky. From this distance it looked the size of a football, and its surface swirled with patterns and coloured shapes.

'It looks small,' she whispered.

'It's bigger from up close,' said Oleander.

'So she's the cat?' Asked Humble.

'We think so.'

'I'd have thought the cat of legend would be more – magical looking – or warrior-ish – you know, not quite so fluffy.'

'Do you mind? I'm standing right here!' Complained Milly.

'Sorry,' said Humble. 'So how is she going to get up there in the sky?'

'She doesn't have to,' said Dan, and explained to Humble what they knew about the true orb being hidden in the mountain.

'This path,' said Humble. 'Has it got a name?'

Dan nodded. 'The way of the three blind mice.'

Milly couldn't help laughing, which made the mice look at her strangely.

'Sorry,' she said.

The mice kept staring and she stopped laughing.

After several awkward moments Humble turned back to Dan

and Oleander. 'There are rumours of a path of that name,' he glanced at Milly. 'Dark rumours – not funny ones at all.'

'The book mentioned some stuff,' Dan agreed vaguely.

Milly felt she needed to explain herself. 'It's just that 'three blind mice' is a nursery rhyme in my world.'

'What's a nursery rhyme?' Asked Humble.

'A sort of poem – for children,' Milly answered.

'And what happens to the mice in your poem?' He asked, with a piercing look.

'Um – they get their tails cut off,' said Milly.

'And you think that's funny?' Asked Humble.

'I suppose not,' said Milly.

Humble turned back to Dan again. 'When are you planning on setting off?'

'As soon as possible,' said Dan.

There was a sudden boom – and a gout of extra thick black smoke puffed out of the top of the mountain.

'Or, maybe now,' Dan went on.

'Probably best,' agreed Humble.

Dan, Oleander and Milly made their way back to the Hanging Cat tavern. Dan produced backpacks for each of them and said he'd packed them with food and other things that might come in useful. Milly's was the biggest and she wondered if she was carrying most of the 'useful' stuff. But she pulled it on and didn't complain, and a few minutes later they were ready to go.

They left the town the way they came in, through the big gates. As the guards hauled them open, Milly thought they looked creaky and old. The guards shouted goodbye and good luck as they headed away down the road outside.

'I've been thinking,' said Milly as they walked along. 'Can't we just shift to where this true orb thingy is – without bothering with the dangerous path?'

Oleander shook her head. 'We can only shift to somewhere we know – either because we've been there already ourselves – or because someone else has shared their thoughts so we can visualise it.'

Milly nodded. That made sense. She remembered Dan saying he'd been able to shift to her world because the Weasel had put it into his head.

'And there's another problem with shifting,' Dan added. 'Do you remember how the rats knew that we'd arrived outside the temple?'

Milly nodded for Dan to continue.

'I think that was because the ninja rat with the staff sensed it when we shifted to the temple. And if he could do that once, he could do it again. Then the rats would know exactly where we were.'

Milly groaned, that didn't sound good. She decided to change the subject. 'Can I ask something about this 'three blind mice' path?'

'You're not going to start laughing again, are you?' Asked Dan.

'No,' Milly said, slightly flustered, then saw Dan grinning and realised he was teasing her.

'No – I just wondered why it was called that?'

Oleander answered. 'The page, that *someone* ripped out of a priceless book, said that there was something at the end of the path that no mouse should ever see.'

'What was it?' Asked Milly.

'Well, given the name of the path, it can't be good... but if *someone* had taken the time to tear out the next page too, that might have told us what it was.'

'I wouldn't have thought you'd approve of *someone* tearing another page out of a library book?' Said Dan.

Oleander glanced sternly at him. 'Well, as the book was ruined already – what would another page have mattered?'

The three of them lapsed into an uncomfortable silence. Oleander was cross again about the book. Dan was cross that she was cross. Milly decided that she would be cross too because she didn't want to be left out.

After another half an hour of walking it seemed to Milly that they were getting further and further away from the temple. Surely they should be heading towards it, not away from it? She was about to break the silence and ask why when the road reached the top of a small rise and she saw the view down into valley below the mountain.

'Oh wow!' She gasped. The road they were following wound away down a slope and then along a thin bridge that went off into the distance, held up by long stone pillars that dropped out of sight for hundreds of feet to the valley floor far below. On the bridge, which was still some way off, she could see tiny figures.

Dan held out his paws to signal them to stop.

'Those are the rats guarding the bridge,' he said.

'Hundreds of them,' agreed Oleander.

'We're not going that way, are we?' Asked Milly. She didn't want to get chased or locked up again.

Dan shook his head.

'No, we take a path off to the left soon, but I think we should get off the road now so none of the soldiers see us.'

Dan led them onto the rocky ground to the side of the road. There were small bushes dotted around, and they tried to creep from one to the other to stay out of sight. Milly was pretty sure that none of the soldiers would be able see them from down on the bridge, but she still moved carefully and quietly.

After ten minutes of creeping, they came to a path that cut across the hillside.

'This looks like it,' said Dan.

They turned left and followed the path. The bridge was far behind them now and they moved more quickly, no longer worried about being spotted.

They came to a dark wood which the path disappeared into. Amongst the dense trees the day immediately seemed colder and gloomier. Milly shivered as they continued along the path. After ten minutes the mice stopped and sniffed the air.

'What's wrong?' Asked Milly. Something about their behaviour was making the fur on her neck stand up.

'Something... evil,' said Oleander.

'What?' Asked Milly, looking around at the dark landscape of tree trunks on both sides of the path. There were tumbles of undergrowth between the trees that looked thorny and forbidding. Only a few lonely shafts of sunlight made it through the canopy of leaves above.

'We must hurry!' Said Dan, and he scurried away along the path.

'It's not far...!' He started to call back, but then Milly's fur was ruffled as something flew past her. Dan disappeared as a large shape flopped down on top of him.

'Dan!' Screamed Oleander.

The shape leapt up from the ground and Dan was gone.

'What was that?' Gasped Milly.

'An owl!' Wailed Oleander.

What? Thought Milly. Just a silly owl? She grabbed Oleander and threw her onto her back.

'Hold on!' She shouted, then launched herself off at a run. She watched the shadow that had snatched Dan as it flapped higher and higher. Luckily it followed the path for a short while, allowing Milly to keep pace with it, but then it veered off to the side. Milly didn't hesitate, she leapt into the thorny undergrowth.

'Ouch....ouch.... ouch....ouch...' Oleander kept squeaking from up on Milly's back as thorns snagged at her fur. But Milly didn't notice them, she was too busy watching the great flapping shape as it wheeled through the canopy above and finally landed on a branch way up in a high tree. Milly hit the tree at a dead run, and used her claws to scramble straight up its rough trunk.

'Whoooooaaaa!' Cried Oleander. Milly could feel her little paws clutching onto the fur round her neck. Milly reached the branch where the great owl was perched just in time. It was dangling poor Dan from its talons and deciding which part of him to eat first. Why wasn't he fighting back? He seemed to be hypnotised by the owl's huge round eyes.

Milly hissed, and the owl turned its head in surprise.

'Too wit, too woo,' it hooted. 'And who are you?'

'Put my friend down!' Spat Milly.

The owl put his head on one side. 'I don't think so, this is my lunch.'

The owl took a breath to say something else, probably something like 'Get out of my tree', or 'And you're my pudding'. But instead, what came out was 'Waaaah!'. Because at that point Milly had pounced on the great fat feathery thing.

The owl fell off the branch in a flurry of feathers and plummeted out of sight. Luckily Milly had already grabbed Dan from the owl's talons before it fell.

Dan came out of his hypnotized daze.

'Milly!' He exclaimed.

Milly smiled with relief and put him up on her back with Oleander. Then she turned around and started walking along the branch back towards the trunk of the tree.

'You didn't need to save me,' Dan said, as he clung onto her fur. 'I had that owl right where I wanted it'.

'It was about to bite your head off,' said Milly.

'It was lucky you turned up before I hurt it,' Dan went on.

'Really?' Said Oleander. 'Well, I'm going to say thank you to Milly, even if you won't. Owls are very dangerous to mice.'

Dan muttered that he'd been about to teach the owl a lesson, but Milly wasn't listening as she'd reached the trunk of the tree and was looking down at the forest floor.

'Do you know how to get down?' Asked Oleander nervously.

'Of course, I'm a cat.' Said Milly as she started edging down the trunk slowly. But then her paws started slipping and she went faster and faster, until she realised she was actually falling.

'Oops,' she said.

Just then a large feathery shape appeared below them and just about had time to say. 'Aha – Got you now!' Before Milly hit the shape and hung on with her claws.

'Waaaah!' Said the owl for the second time that day.

The mixture of fur and feathers plunged down through the branches, Milly hanging on tight and the owl squawking and fluttering and trying to fly.

'Oooof!' Said the owl finally, as they hit the ground with it underneath.

Milly and the mice scrambled up leaving the dazed owl lying on the forest floor.

'Ooooow...' The owl moaned.

They watched it warily, but it didn't get up, so they slowly crept away into the undergrowth.

They soon found the path again and continued following it. This time Dan kept glancing nervously up into the gloomy dark of the canopy above. The path took them winding through the wood, deeper and deeper, until it suddenly stopped when it reached a rocky wall.

'Oh!' Said Milly. 'Did we come the wrong way?'

'No,' said Dan. He peered at the wall, looking around for something. Oleander helped by looking as well. Milly watched the two mice.

'I'm hungry, can we stop here and eat something?' She asked. Even the dried fish in her backpack seemed like a good idea to her rumbling stomach.

'Not here, there might be more owls, let's get inside first,' said Dan.

'Inside where?' Said Milly, looking at the solid rocky wall.

As if in answer to her question, a large rock about Milly's height suddenly moved on its own. Dan and Oleander jumped back as it rocked towards them and then slammed onto the ground.

'Hey – that nearly got my paw!' Complained Milly.

Behind where the rock had fallen was a dark opening in the hillside.

'Come on', said Dan, and took them into a rocky-walled passageway. It was very dark, and even Milly's cat eyes couldn't see where it led.

Dan rummaged in his pack and pulled something out, and a second later Milly could see again in the dull glow of a stick-shaped thing Dan held in his paw. He passed similar stick-shaped things to her and Oleander. Oleander bashed one end of hers on the ground, and it started to glow too. Milly copied her and then held the stick up to look at more closely. It felt like it was made of wood, but the whole length of it glowed with a dim grey light that didn't give off any heat.

'Ghost sticks,' said Oleander, with a slight shudder. 'Where did you get these?'

'My friend at the Hanging Cat,' he said.

'What makes them glow?' Asked Milly. There was something fascinating about them, almost tasty, which was odd.

'Souls of dead rats,' said Dan.

Nice, thought Milly.

'Shall we stop and have that break for food you asked for?' Asked Dan.

'Actually, I'm suddenly not hungry,' said Milly.

A scraping noise made her glance back at the entrance. Outside, the huge rock that had nearly fallen on her paw was wobbling. Almost as though it was alive. As she watched it rolled slowly upright and then slammed back against the mouth of the passageway. It made them all jump.

'What was that!' Gasped Oleander.

'The rock,' Milly pointed at the entrance, which was now sealed up tight. She was glad to have the ghost sticks now as without them it would have been pitch black.

'That was weird,' said Dan. 'I suppose there's only one way to go now.'

With that, he turned and started off along the dark passageway holding his ghost stick in front of him.

9

The Path Under the Mountain

Milly started to hear thumping, crashing, sounds as she followed Dan and Oleander. To start with they sounded very quiet and far away. But slowly they became louder, especially as they turned corners in the passageway. They came every thirty seconds or so, although some were more often, and Milly found herself jumping every time one sounded.

'Er, what's that sound?' She asked, as it seemed like anytime now they would reach whatever was making it.

'I expect it's the first challenge,' said Dan.

'Challenge?' Asked Milly.

'Yes, the page from the book said there are challenges to face on this path,' explained Oleander.

'As well as the thing at the end that no one's ever meant to see?'

Oleander nodded over her shoulder in the dim light of the ghost sticks.

'No one mentioned any challenges,' grumbled Milly, as they rounded a bend and the thumping noises got really loud.

Whatever it was, they were nearly there.

And around the next bend Milly saw she was right. The passage went under a stone arch and beyond was a great hallway, about thirty paces square, with a high ceiling. There seemed to be light coming from somewhere, so they all banged their ghost sticks to switch them off and put them away in their packs. Large, square stone columns were spaced around the hall, which Milly thought were holding up the ceiling, until one started to rise up off the floor. She watched amazed as it went up out of sight into a slot in the ceiling.

'What...?' She started.

Crash! In another part of the hall a different stone column came crashing down from of the ceiling and hit the floor.

'Oh my goodness!' She cried.

'Those columns are big crushers,' gasped Oleander.

'How are we going to get across to the other side?' Wondered Dan.

There was another archway at the far side of the hall, where the passageway under the mountain looked like it continued onwards.

They all stood and watched for a few minutes. Columns rumbled back up into the ceiling randomly, and more columns came crashing down elsewhere. Milly couldn't work out any pattern to it.

'We'll have to try walking across,' breathed Dan. 'And hope for the best.'

'That's a joke, I assume?' Said Oleander.

'There's no other way – it all seems completely random.'

'But if one comes down on top of us, we'll be crushed,' whispered Milly.

'We've got no choice,' Dan said. 'I'll go first.'

And Dan just walked out into the hall.

'Dan!' Oleander cried out. But Dan kept going.

Milly held her breath.

He went four paces... five... six... seven... nearly a quarter of the way across the hall.

Then there was a quiet click... and a column crashed down. Had it hit him? Milly couldn't see him anymore.

'Nooo,' wailed Oleander.

Milly stared at the column. Would blood start oozing out from underneath? Then Dan's head poked around the side of it and he called out. 'That was close.'

'Come back here!' Shouted Oleander, as three more columns smashed down in quick succession in other parts of the hall.

'I can't, I'm stuck!' Dan yelled back. 'The column's on the end of my tail.'

He sounded very scared. Milly gulped and dashed out into the hall. She had to save him. Almost immediately two more columns crashed down near the archway on the far side of the hall, making her jump sideways even though they were nowhere near her. And then another column smashed down on the stone where she'd just been standing.

She skittered round in front of the column that had trapped Dan's tail.

He was shocked she'd come out into the hallway. 'What are you doing here? I can't move until this column goes back up.'

But Milly had another idea. 'What about if I bite off the end of your tail?'

'It's the only tail I've got...' started Dan. Then a column crashed down very close to them. It seemed like they could sense where they were.

Dan shuddered and closed his eyes. 'All right then – do it.'

Milly bent her head down, opened her mouth, and... creeeeak... the column moved up off the floor and Dan's tail was free.

'Quick,' Dan pulled Milly directly under the rising column. What was he was doing? And then the four columns all around them suddenly crashed down.

'What did you do that for?' Gasped Milly. 'Now we're trapped.

They were both squeezed onto a single flagstone with stone columns all around.

'I thought we'd be safe under a column that was still going up,' said Dan. 'I didn't know this would happen.'

Above them, the column that had trapped Dan's tail was still rumbling back up into the roof.

Dan and Milly watched it go up. Somehow there was still light to see, and Milly realised that the columns themselves were glowing slightly.

'What if it comes straight back down again?' She asked.

'Then we won't know much about it,' said Dan grimly. 'But we'd better be ready to run the moment any of these other columns move.'

They waited and waited, hearing columns crashing down elsewhere in the hall, until it started to feel like the one above them could come hammering down at any time.

Some dust fell from above and Milly cringed, but then there was a grinding sound and one of the columns next to them started going up.

Dan scampered under it as soon as it was mouse-height off the floor. Thanks, thought Milly, just leave me. She had to wait another second before she could squeeze underneath and, as she did that, a rush of air blew her sideways as the column they'd been stuck under finally crashed down. That was it! She ran! So fast that she overtook Dan and scooped him up on her way back to the archway. Milly had never been so relieved as when she got back to the safety of the passageway.

'Phew,' she gasped, as they leaned against the wall to get their breath back.

Then Milly realised something was wrong. Oleander was nowhere to be seen.

'Oleander, where are you!' Dan's voice sounded desperate as he shouted out. Milly looked all around, expecting the young queen to step out from behind a rock.

'Yoo-hoo!'

Milly spun around to peer across the hall of columns.

On the far side Oleander was waving from the other archway.

'What are you doing over there?' Shouted Dan.

'I came to try and help,' Oleander called back. 'But then you disappeared, and I got scared and just ran.'

'Why didn't *we* run that way?' Wondered Milly.

For some reason the columns seemed to have stopped crashing down, and the ones they could see all rumbled back into the ceiling. Soon it was quiet and there were no columns to be seen at all. It felt like they were just waiting for Milly and Dan to try to cross again.

'Maybe we should do what Oleander did, and just run as fast as we can,' suggested Dan.

'Okay,' Milly said slowly. 'Who's first?'

Dan looked at her.

'Both together?' He suggested. Milly thought for a bit, gulped, then nodded. They crouched and got ready to run.

A minute later they were still crouching.

Milly glanced sideways at Dan. 'We've got to go sometime.'

'Okay, I'll count to three,' said Dan.

Oleander was watching from the other side, a paw over her

mouth. She looked even more scared than they were.

'One.... Two.... Three!'

Dan scampered forwards and Milly followed.

Crash! The first column smashed down right in front of Milly. She jumped sideways and kept running.

Crash! A column nearly got Dan's tail again but he was running too fast.

Crash! Dan went nose-first into a column that came down in front of him, stopped dazed for a moment, then shook his head and skittered round it quickly, just in time before a column crashed down where he'd just been standing.

Crash! Crash! Columns came down to the left and right of Milly but she kept on running. Crash! Another one nearly got her right paw and she jumped away sideways. Crash! One nearly got her left paw and she had to jump the other way.

Milly was totally confused now and didn't know which direction was the way out. She just kept running.

'Made it!' She heard Dan shout. But that had come from behind her! She spun round and ran in that direction.

Crash! Another column came down in front of her, scraping her nose and cutting her off. She scampered to her left.

Crash! Crash! Crash! Three columns came down in a line, and her only option was to run along the side of them.

So many columns had come done now the hallway was like a maze, and she could no longer see the walls or the arches, just columns. She weaved between them, praying she wouldn't hit a dead end.

Crash! She slid to a halt as a column that seemed larger than the rest came down in front of her.

Crash! Crash! Crash! Before she could move three more columns came down all around her. She found herself trapped again, like she had been with Dan before. She looked up fearfully, there must be a column above her just waiting to come down and crush her flat.

The flagstone she was standing on seemed bigger than the others in the hall, and it was carved... with bones, and skulls. Not a good sign, she thought. Something told her that she was at the very middle of the hallway.

A voice from right next to her made her jump. 'Quick – take my paw!'

It was Dan!

She grabbed his paw but then something up above clicked. The column was coming! Milly squeezed her eyes shut.

Crash!

After a few seconds Milly wondered why being crushed didn't hurt. And why she could still feel the floor under her paws. And why she was still breathing.

She opened her eyes slowly.

Dan was holding her paw and they were standing under a stone archway. Oleander was in front of her, looking relieved and afraid at the same time. She was out from under those awful columns!

Milly turned round to look back into the hallway. The columns were standing like a forest so that she couldn't see across to the other side. But even as she watched they started to rumble up one by one back into the roof.

'What happened?' She asked.

'I shifted you out', explained Dan.

Milly thought about that, she was grateful, but... 'I was nearly crushed... probably a hundred times... and I hurt my nose!'

She rubbed her nose where the column had scraped it. 'Why didn't you shift us across that terrible hallway in the first place?'

Dan looked worried. 'Like I said before that ninja rat may be out there somewhere, waiting for us to shift so he can sense where we are.'

Milly paused to think about that. 'Does that matter?'

Dan nodded. 'If he senses where we are, he could shift here, and bring more rats with him.'

In the hall the columns had now all risen into the roof and it was quiet.

'We'd better get going, then,' said Milly.

'Yes,' agreed Dan. 'As quickly as we can.'

In the courtyard of the temple a large rat sat on the ground at its centre. He was in everyone's way, but the other rats walked around him carefully. He had black wiry fur and grasped a staff in one grimy paw. At the end of the staff a round orb the size of a small ball hovered in a loop of wood. The orb looked like a miniature version of the great orb above the temple.

An old rat Sergeant watched the big rat warily as he took a break munching some cheese at the side of the courtyard. A smaller rat came up to him, with bandages around his head, and pointed over at the big rat.

'What's that all about, Sarge?' He asked.

The older rat finished chewing a piece of cheese. 'That, young Ember, is a ninja rat – from up in the mountains – they're grow big up there, they do.'

'What's it doing?'

'Some sort of magic. Ninja rats can do that, you know. Just like the temple mice.'

At that point Mordred stamped into the courtyard and all the rat soldiers jumped to attention. The rat Sergeant hid his cheese and stopped chewing, and watched Mordred go across to the ninja rat and shout. 'Have you found them yet?'

The ninja rat just opened one eye and looked up.

'Well?' Added Mordred.

The rat stood up slowly. He wore a leather belt around his middle, and more belts over his shoulders. Hanging off the belts were ninja weapons, lots of them. There were knives and swords and spiky round throwing-things and chains with balls attached. And even scarier, the orb on the end of his staff swirled with dark colours and a network of sparks.

'Nothing…,' said the rat. 'I sense nothing… no mouse magic…

no shifting. Those mice are smart, and scared... they've run away.'

'They won't have,' asserted Mordred. 'They'll still be around somewhere – they're probably hiding in the town.'

'I can go to the town if you want – I'll take my brothers. No-one there can stand against us, and it won't take us long to find someone that will tell us where they're hiding.'

Mordred hesitated and looked suspicious for a moment. The sergeant wasn't surprised, he'd be suspicious of those ninja rat brothers as well. Especially now they had those magic staffs. He imagined them down in the town, plotting how they could take over Mordred's rat army.

'No,' said Mordred finally. 'If they're hiding in the town, they can't do anything – and they'll be killed by the eruption anyway, along with everyone else.'

The sergeant glanced up at the smoking mountain. He didn't much like the idea of it erupting. Would they all have time to get out?

Suddenly the ninja rat stiffened and sniffed the air. The patterns on the orb in his staff swirled more wildly.

'Got you!' He muttered to himself.

'What was that?' Barked Mordred.

'Someone just shifted... I know where they are, now!'

'Then take some soldiers and go and kill them!' Shouted Mordred with glee. 'Kill them! Kill them! Kill them!'

'No, I can do this on my own.'

Mordred looked shocked. 'Are you sure?'

The rat sneered. 'Don't worry, I'll bring you back their skins.'

And the air shimmered as he disappeared.

Milly, Dan and Oleander were about to hurry away from the hall of columns when the air shimmered at its centre and a black rat appeared.

'Oh no...' Breathed Milly.

The rat smiled when he saw them, with dirty, broken teeth.

Oleander saw the weapons on his belts and sensed his wiry strength. Dan saw the staff he was carrying and felt the waves of its power. Milly saw the rat's dirty, matted fur, and caught a whiff of its smell.

They all started to back away along the passageway behind them.

'Don't move!' Snarled the rat and pointed his staff, sending sparks and swirls of purple light leaping out towards them.

Milly felt her legs go weak and she fell to the ground. Dan and Oleander slumped down next to her.

The rat pulled out a wicked looking knife from his belt. 'I promised someone your skins.'

Milly stared at the awful knife. The blade was a strange, ornate shape and glittered with a red sheen like blood.

The rat giggled at her. 'A fluffy cat, if I'm not mistaken, your skin will make a nice coat for winter...'

He moved one leg to step forwards, then...

Crash!

Milly blinked. One instant the rat had been there, gloating and smirking, and the next instant he was gone. In the space where he'd been standing the large central column looked as solid as if it had always been there. The rat's staff clattered down in front of the column and the sparks and swirls of light from it faded away. Milly felt pins and needles in her legs as they came back to life.

Oleander gasped. 'Oh my goodness!'

Dan gave a long whistle of relief. 'Oh dear... poor rat... Never mind.'

Oleander put a paw to her mouth. 'Was he... crushed?'

'Completely splattered,' confirmed Milly.

'Flat as a pancake,' agreed Dan.

'But why did he shift there, under that big column?' Asked Oleander.

Dan shrugged. 'When I shifted to save Milly, that's where I went to... he must've sensed that, and then just shifted to the same place.'

'Poor rat,' said Oleander, but she actually sounded like she really meant it.

'Serves it right. It was going to kill us,' reminded Dan.

They all went silent. They'd had a lucky escape. Oleander gazed at the floor of the hall. 'Is that an elder's staff?'

Dan nodded. 'Looks like it.'

He took off his backpack and rummaged inside, then pulled out a rope. He quickly tied a loop in its end and threw it across the hall. The loop landed on top of the staff.

'Yes,' breathed Dan.

He twitched the rope a couple of times, until the loop caught on the orb at the end of the staff.

Then he pulled the rope back very slowly, dragging the staff along with it.

'Thank you, Mordred!' He muttered, as it got close enough for him to reach and grab it. He stroked the wood of the staff and stared at its orb, then smiled in delight. He turned to Oleander.

'I think it's your staff,' he said, and held it out to her.

She took the staff slowly. 'I can't believe I have this back,' she breathed.

As she looked into the orb the colours swirled faster.

'What is it?' Asked Milly.

'The staff of healing,' she said. 'The wood is very old and has powerful magic which creates a reflection of the orb at its end.'

Milly was fascinated by the colours in the orb. 'What does it do?'

Oleander stood straighter and set the end of the staff on the ground. 'It gives me back my magic!'

10

Cavern of Monsters

With her staff back, Oleander seemed more confident. She took the lead, heading off down the passageway away from the hallway of columns with her head high, and the staff held out in front of her, the orb at its tip shining bright and lighting the way.

'Does this mean she's more magic than you now?' Whispered Milly to Dan.

Dan smiled. 'The queen was always more magic than me. The staff of healing makes her more powerful still.'

'Healing? But how will that help with fighting rats?' Asked Milly.

Dan chuckled. 'Wait and see.'

Oleander glanced over her shoulder. 'It will certainly help if one of us gets hurt. There are five staffs. The others are the staff of wisdom, the staff of making, the staff of nature and the staff of conquest.'

'And do they belong to the elders?' asked Milly.

Dan nodded. 'Yes. Or at least they did, it seems like Mordred's given them to his ninja rats now.'

They all walked on in silence for a while. Milly was thinking about everything that had happened. She remembered that Dan had said the columns were only the first challenge.

'Is there another challenge?' She asked Dan.

'The book said there were three,' Dan replied, then slowed as Oleander stopped ahead of them.

Oleander had come to a halt where the passageway widened out into a round room. Milly and Dan caught up with her and found it wasn't a room at all. It had no floor, just a hole that dropped away into blackness. Milly glanced around the walls; there were no other passageways leading out.

'Where do we go now?' She asked.

Oleander and Dan shrugged; they didn't know any more than she did.

'Maybe it's a puzzle,' she suggested, and started searching around the walls of the passageway near the hole, pressing anything that looked like it might move.

'What are you doing?' Asked Dan.

'There might be a secret button.'

Dan laughed. 'That's not very likely.'

Click! A piece of rock moved under Milly's paw.

'Oh,' said Dan.

There was grinding sound and Milly looked around to see what was moving, feeling very pleased with herself.

The grinding sound kept going, but none of them could see what was causing it. Then Milly glanced behind her and saw that a wall was coming down from the roof, blocking their way back.

'Oh dear,' she said.

Dan turned round and saw the wall too. 'Yes... Oh dear.'

The wall got down floor level and the grinding sound stopped.

'I will open it with my staff!' Oleander said grandly and pointed her staff at the wall.

'Open!' She commanded.

The grinding sound started up again and Oleander smiled. But then they saw the wall wasn't going back up, it was slowly moving towards them!

'Oh dear,' said Oleander.

'We already said that,' said Dan.

The wall got closer and closer, pushing them backwards towards the edge of the hole.

Milly leaned her shoulder against it, trying to stop it moving. The mice did the same. Their paws slithered backwards as the wall continued to push them. Milly's back left paw scrabbled in empty space

'Eek,' she cried.

The wall didn't stop, it kept pushing.

'Noooo...' she cried, as she overbalanced and fell into the blackness of the hole.

Milly fell and fell, wind scraping her fur flat, and for ages she couldn't see a thing. Then a faint light grew below her, and a shape that got bigger and bigger. A great open mouth, in a face with slanted eyes, and wicked fangs, lit up by a shaft of sunlight that came in from somewhere.

'Helpppp!' Yelled Milly, as she dropped into the wide-open mouth. Even though she saw the mouth was carved out of stone, it felt like she'd been swallowed whole.

'Ooof,' she said as she finally hit something. But it didn't really hurt, it was more of a surprise. It felt like she had hit the side of the wall and bounced off. Moments later she hit it again, then again, and again, in closer and closer succession.

Finally, she hit it and stuck, and she felt like she was sliding. She decided that the hole must have slowly turned until it was slanted, becoming like a slide in a gigantic dark funfair. Suddenly a sideways curve flung her one way, and then another flung her the other way. It was still completely dark, but it seemed like the slide was getting less steep.

More light appeared ahead, and suddenly she zoomed into an open cavern. Again, light was somehow coming in from outside, but there was no time to see where from. She was still going very fast, and at the end of the cavern Milly could see that the slide branched into three separate tunnels. The right hand one was carved like an open, scaly mouth, the middle one was carved with leaping flames and the left hand one was carved with hairy feet with huge claws. What a choice! She threw her weight to the right and shot away down the tunnel carved with the open mouth.

It went dark again, and the slide zoomed around two final steep curves, and then the floor of the slide evened out and she slowed down. Just as she thought everything was going to be all right the slide ended and she went head over paws into the darkness and thumped into some kind of odd wall, ending up in a heap.

Milly lay there for a second, then pushed herself up onto her paws. She'd just stood up when she was knocked over by two flying mice.

'That felt like Milly,' came a squeak in the darkness.

'Yes, nice and soft,' came another squeak.

'Thanks for knocking me over,' said Milly. She knew from their voices it was Dan and Oleander.

'You're welcome... I wonder where we are,' said Dan.

'There's a funny smell,' said Oleander as she made her staff glow softly so they could see.

'I'm amazed we all ended up in the same place,' said Milly.

'Yes,' said Dan. 'Lucky we all chose the same tunnel back there.'

'Yes, the one with the big scary mouth just seemed to be the right one,' agreed Milly.

'Oh, I chose the one with the fire,' said Dan.

'And I chose the one with the claws,' said Oleander.

'Oh,' said Dan again. 'Maybe it's someone's idea of a joke, since all the tunnels led to the same place.'

'No,' said Oleander. 'There was something about it on that torn page.'

Her face was lit up by a glow her orb.

'It mentioned three choices,' she went on. 'A challenge with three choices where you must choose the nature of your doom.'

They all thought about that for a moment.

'And we all chose a different tunnel?' Asked Milly.

The two mice nodded.

'So does that mean we will have to face all three dooms?' She asked.

And at that moment, a loud and angry roar shattered the still, dark air of the cavern.

Milly peered out into the dark towards where the sound came from. But all she could make out in the glow from Oleander's staff was the strange wall next to them and a rock covered floor. She couldn't even see the slide that they'd shot down when they arrived.

'Should I make the light brighter?' Asked Oleander.

No one said anything. Milly desperately wanted to see more but standing in the only pool of light in this dark space made her feel that eyes were watching her.

Dan spoke first. 'If that sound was some kind of monster, then it must be able to see us... I think we should turn the light off altogether.'

He was right, thought Milly, but the idea of groping around in the darkness while monsters were hunting them filled her with dread. 'But what if we lose each other?'

Dan reached out. 'Let's all hold paws – and then follow this wall along.'

Milly looked at the wall, it was solid but didn't seem to be made from rock, instead it was smooth and black, and in places clumps of hair grew out of it like strange underground plants.

'Which way?' Asked Oleander, her voice a squeaky whisper.

Before anyone could answer, the roar sounded again, closer.

'That way!' Whispered Milly, pointing to the right, the opposite direction from where the roar had come from.

Milly took hold of Dan's paw, then grabbed Oleander's. 'You go first,' she said to Dan.

'Okay,' he replied, reaching his free paw to touch the wall. 'Now, switch off the light.'

Oleander's orb dimmed to nothing and it became pitch black again.

Milly felt Dan's paw tug, and she followed where he led. The ground was rocky, and she had to be careful not to stumble. None of them spoke, so whatever was roaring in the darkness wouldn't hear them.

At first it seemed to work, as the next roar sounded further away. They tried to go more quickly, but it was very difficult not to trip over on the rocky ground. The wall they were following went on and on.

Roar! Grrrr! Argghhh!

Dan froze and Milly bumped into him. The noise was suddenly very close.

Grrr! Warrghhh! Roaaaaar!

A wave of stinky monster breath washed over Milly, and she felt Dan let go of her. There was a rummaging sound and then a small bang, and suddenly she could see again in the light of Dan's ghost stick.

Milly looked fearfully upwards for a huge monster.

'Wheeeeere is it?' She whispered, her voice shivering.

'I don't know,' said Dan, waving the ghost stick to shed light into the darkness.

Oleander tugged Milly's paw. 'Right there in front of us.'

Milly lowered her gaze and there, sitting up on its back legs facing them, was a green and gold lizard. Its face was the same as that carved on the tunnels, and the mouth the same as they'd dropped through as they fell down the hole.

Milly smiled in relief. 'It sounded bigger.' It was only about the same size as her.

The lizard opened its mouth.

Roarrrrr! Whooaragh! Argghghgh! And the stinky breath washed over them again.

They all backed against the wall, suddenly scared again. The lizard crouched down then leapt, its mouth opening impossibly wide. It was like a cave had opened in front of them with teeth like huge scary stalactites hanging down. They scrambled away in different directions, moving as fast as only terrified cats and mice can. The lizard missed them and crashed into the wall. For a moment it was dazed, then it spun around looking for them. Milly watched in horror as it opened its mouth again, wider and wider. That mouth could swallow them all whole!

But then the wall behind the lizard moved.

'Eeerough?' The lizard snapped its mouth shut, then sniffed the air and looked around. It almost seemed scared. But then it shook its head, fixed its gaze on Milly, and started to open its great mouth again.

'Crump!'

One moment the lizard was about to attack, and the next a huge fat foot had come out of the darkness to land on top of it. An enormous hairy face appeared above the foot. It was not a cute face. It had squinty black eyes, a piggy looking snout, and a mouth so full of dirty teeth that they stuck out in odd directions. Gloopy saliva dribbled down its chin.

'Yuck!' Said Milly.

The big piggy nose snuffled and twitched, and then suddenly sneezed.

'Double Yuck,' said Oleander, as she was hit by strings of slime.

Milly realised that the wall they had been following hadn't

been a wall at all, but the side of a huge pig-like monster.

Another hairy paw appeared out of the darkness and wiped its snout, and then its black piggy eyes focused on them again.

'Snorrt!'

It lunged at them with its toothy mouth open to snuffle them up.

🐷 🐷 🐷

Milly, Dan and Oleander scrambled backwards as fast as they could. But the slimy snout kept coming, sniffing at the ground, seeming to follow their scent. The monster's eyes were squinted half shut, even in the dull glow of Dan's glow stick. It gave Milly an idea.

'Oleander!' She gasped. 'Could your staff make a really bright light?'

'Yes,' said Oleander. 'But how will that help?'

'Its eyes are used to the dark... a bright light might hurt them and give us a chance to get away.'

'Yes – do it!' Huffed Dan.

'Everyone close your eyes!' Shouted Oleander.

The sudden light from Oleander's orb was so bright it flashed redness even through Milly's closed eyelids.

A huge squeal sounded, followed by the noise of large limbs scrabbling about. Milly opened their eyes again. Oleander had dimmed her staff to a soft glow. The monster was nowhere to be seen, but Milly could hear it thumping around somewhere away in the darkness.

'Make it lighter,' Dan hissed.

Oleander nodded and the glow got brighter and brighter until they could see the pig monster rolling around with its hairy claws scrabbling at its eyes, still squealing in pain.

'Let's go,' whispered Dan.

They turned and started to creep away. Milly was still very scared. They'd been lucky so far, but she couldn't help wondering what the third doom was. The two monsters they'd faced so far seemed to match the carvings of the fanged mouth and hairy claws back on that slide-thing, so would there be a fire monster as well?

The squealing sounds became fainter as they hurried away, able to go faster now with Oleander's brighter light to see be.

Milly kept looking around in every direction, searching for signs of a way out of this huge cave, as well as looking out for any third monster.

'Thank goodness!' Breathed Oleander. Finally, a rocky wall had appeared ahead of them, and set into it was a huge archway with a gate made of iron bars.

Milly's heart sank, the gaps between the bars were tiny, and didn't look big enough for a cat to squeeze through. They reached the gates and stared up at them. Milly grabbed one of the gates and pushed and pulled it. There was no movement at all, it was locked up tight.

'What now?' She asked in despair.

As they all stood silently and gazed at the gate, Milly realised that the piggy squeals had stopped. She hoped the pig monster had gone away, too scared to chase them anymore. But then loud thumping scrabbling noises started up again, coming their way.

'Oh no!' Breathed Milly. She looked back at the bars. 'You two could squeeze through,' she said bravely to the mice. 'There's no point in all of us getting snuffled up.'

The two mice shook their heads.

'No – we'll stay with you and fight it,' said Dan. At the same time Oleander planted the end of her staff in the ground. Did she have any other magic that could help them? The huge pig came into view, moving slower than last time, it's snout on the ground and its eyes screwed tightly shut.

It was searching for them by smell, thought Milly. Oleander's bright light wouldn't save them this time. But even so, a new flickering light suddenly bathed everything in a yellow glow.

'It's no good Oleander,' Milly said. 'That thing's got its eyes shut now.'

'Err, it's not me,' said Oleander.

Milly stopped staring at the pig monster and looked around to see where the yellow light was coming from. High up above them a long trail of fire twisted and turned in the air as it swirled downwards.

Great! Thought Milly. Now there's a fire monster too.

The fiery thing was beautiful. Like a long sinuous string of flames, it weaved patterns in the darkness. Milly felt waves of heat ruffle her fur as it swirled towards them. It seemed in no hurry to attack, but it was getting lower and lower. It was yellow and orange and white, completely made of fire that streamed out behind it. She could see no mouth, or legs, or wings.

'Oink!'

Milly's head spun back to look in front of her. The pig monster was almost on top of them, its big hairy face pointed down at the ground, its snout still moving back and forth. As it got close it stilled, seeming to sense exactly where they were. Then it reared up, opened its awful toothy mouth and lunged down at them.

Milly tried to jump away but knew she was too late. She'd been distracted by the fire snake and now she was going to be eaten by the pig monster!

But then she felt an intense wash of heat and smelled her own fur being singed as something streamed by her, and she saw the fiery snake throw itself into the pig monster's open mouth. The pig monster scrambled backwards away from them and sat down suddenly, looking confused. It shook its head a couple of times, slobber flying everywhere. Then it jumped up and squealed, ran around twice in circles, then threw itself onto its back. The ground shook when it landed.

The poor monster kicked a few times and then lay still. A

smell of cooking bacon wafted past Milly and the mice.

A curve of fire appeared out of one of the pig's nostrils, swirling up gracefully to circle twice around its head. Then it looped and swooped down onto the ground in front of them, where it coiled itself, just like a snake, with one end swaying like a head... watching them.

'Oh dear!' Said Dan.

Oleander stepped forward and pointed her staff.

'Begone you fiery fiend!' She shouted.

Milly felt a rush of hope that Oleander's magic could make it go away.

The fiery head hissed and sizzled, like it was laughing. Then it reared up above Oleander.

'No!' Milly shouted and threw herself at Oleander. She scooped up the mouse and pulled her back to the gate, just as the fiery snake struck. Its head bounced off the rock and instantly rose again searching for its prey. It sizzled forwards across the ground. How could they fight something that had so easily killed the pig monster?

Roaaaaar! Arghghghgh! Weeeraghhh!

What? That was the sound of the lizard again! Was it still alive?

Behind the fiery snake, Milly saw the lizard creep out from the darkness, its mouth opening like a cave again. Then it jumped forwards and its mouth snapped shut over the fire monster. As suddenly as it had appeared, the snake was gone, and there was just the lizard standing there, curls of smoke leaking out from its closed mouth. With a bit of an effort, it swallowed. Gulp!

Milly watched as the lizard shook its head a couple of times, the same as the pig monster had. She actually felt sorry for it, being cooked from the inside out must be horrible. But then the lizard burped loudly and licked its lips. Its eyes focused on Milly and the mice, and it started opening its awful mouth again. Had it really just eaten the fire monster with no problem at all?

There was nowhere to go, Milly and the mice were already backed up against the gate. Milly was about to shout to Oleander and Dan to squeeze through the bars and get away, when the lizard snapped its mouth shut, looked a bit sick, burped, and fell over sideways.

They all stared as it lay squirming on the ground.

'Is it dying?' Asked Oleander.

'I don't know,' replied Dan. 'Let's not wait around to find out... we need to get these gates open.'

Milly agreed. The lizard might recover at any moment, or the fire monster could appear back out of it again. They needed to get away. She saw Oleander squeeze between the bars and hold up her staff to look at the gate from the other side. 'I can see where it's locked from here!' She called. 'I think it's a magic lock.'

'Can you open it?' Milly asked.

'I'll try,' Oleander pointed her staff upwards and frowned in concentration.

'Open!' She commanded, and the orb on her staff swirled with greens and blues.

Nothing happened.

'Errr – please?' She added.

There was a metallic click, then a creaking noise, and one of the barred gates opened a crack.

Milly grabbed the gate and pulled, and although it was stiff, she managed to get it open wide enough to squeeze through.

'Now let's get it shut again,' breathed Dan, who had followed behind her.

Milly grabbed the gate and heaved it closed again, then Oleander stepped back and pointed her staff once more.

'Close... please,' she commanded, having learned her lesson about being polite to gates.

Click!

'Come on,' Dan turned to walk away along a new passageway that led away from the cavern, his ghost stick held high. Then he realised Milly and Oleander hadn't followed him and turned back. They were still watching the lizard through the bars of the gate. It was now rolling around and moaning, small wisps of smoke coming out of its nose.

'Poor thing,' said Oleander.

'It was going to eat us,' Dan reminded her.

'But it's in pain,' said Milly.

'We have to go,' said Dan.

'Can you help it with your staff?' Milly asked Oleander.

Oleander nodded. 'I can try.'

'Did anyone hear me? That thing tried to eat us!' Dan repeated.

'But we're safe now, it's locked on the other side of the gates,' said Milly. 'And it's such a poor thing.'

Oleander held up her staff. She started humming a quiet tune, and the colours of the orb turned violet and creamy white. For a minute or so Oleander's singing didn't seem to have any effect, but then the lizard stopped rolling about so much and after a while it laid still. Just as Milly thought maybe it had died, it gave a huge burp and smoke came out in a cloud, then opened its eyes and looked straight at Oleander. Milly thought it looked grateful. It struggled to its feet and faced them. Oleander stopped singing and brought her staff back to her side.

'There,' she said. 'Better now?'

The lizard paused, then nodded its head.

'It understood!' Said Milly.

'Ahhh,' said Oleander.

Dan made a strangled noise. 'It's a monster remember,' he said as he pulled his backpack over his shoulders again. 'Come on, let's get going.'

Milly and Oleander picked up their backpacks. The lizard was still looking at them. Oleander gave it a small wave as they turned and started walking away.

'It's just a good thing that monster's locked behind those

gates!' Dan said grumpily.

They'd only gone a few steps when they heard a terrible sound.

Click!

They all spun around.

'Err... do you think... we might not have locked the gate properly?' Whispered Oleander.

Creak!

Milly watched in horror as the lizard pulled the gate open and came through into the passageway. It looked around in wonder – was this the first time it had ever been out of that awful cavern?

It stalked towards them, and they backed away. It got closer and closer. Dan got ready to fight. Oleander held up her staff. Milly shivered and her fur fluffed up.

But the lizard didn't open its awful mouth, it edged up to Oleander, and bent its nose down towards her and sniffed. It was much bigger than her, but she bravely reached up a paw and scratched its nose. It nuzzled her fur.

'Well,' said Dan. 'It looks like you've got a new friend.'

11

Facing the Curse

Milly felt a bit strange heading off down the new passageway with the lizard trailing after them. It seemed happy to follow along at the back and didn't show any sign of wanting to eat them anymore. Every once in a while it burped, and seemed surprised when a puff of smoke came out of its mouth. Each time it happened the lizard stopped and watched the smoke as it curled up and away over its head, and then hurried to catch up.

Milly noticed its strange behaviour and decided that it didn't usually burp out puffs of smoke. Had eating the fire monster made it sick?

She was so preoccupied with glancing back at the lizard that she didn't notice when they walked straight into the third challenge.

The lizard suddenly squawked and dashed past them, making them all jump. It threw itself in front of Oleander and snapped something out of the air. When it turned back to look at them it had an arrow grasped between its jaws.

'Woaah!' Dan backed away quickly, pulling Milly and Oleander with him.

'Was that someone shooting at us?' Gasped Milly.

'I don't know,' said Dan glaring along the passageway ahead. 'But I expect it's the third challenge.'

'I don't understand, what are these challenges for?' Asked Milly crossly. She'd really had enough of this.

'The page from the book that got torn out...' Oleander glared at Dan. '... said that the three challenges will ensure that only mice who are worthy can reach the orb.'

'Or cats,' added Milly.

'I hope so,' murmured Dan.

'Hope so!' Exploded Milly. 'Didn't that page say if cats could get through?'

Oleander shook her head. Great, thought Milly.

Behind them the lizard burped out another gout of smoke and dropped the arrow onto the ground. Milly bent and picked it up. It had a wicked metal tip, and the shaft was made of black wood. It had flights made of multi-coloured feathers.

'So where did this come from?' She asked, gazing around at the rocky walls.

Now she looked carefully, she realised the passageway was wider than it had been earlier. And up ahead it widened even more until the walls disappeared into the gloom beyond the light from Oleander's staff.

'Can you make more light?' Milly asked.

Oleander made her staff glow brighter, and it became clear that the passageway turned into a cave ahead of them. The walls of the cave were uneven and rocky, and even in the stronger light there were deep shadows and cracks that could hide anything.

Milly took off her backpack and held it by the straps, then swung it a couple of times and threw it into the cave. It sailed through the air and landed in the middle, and three thunks sounded in quick succession. When the backpack rolled over there were three more black arrows stuck into it.

'How are we going to get through there?' Milly gasped.

They all sat down and thought about it. Milly stared at her backpack laying on the ground of the cave. 'Do you suppose that's it, and there's no more arrows?'

Dan shook his head. 'I doubt it's that easy.'

'Then we're trapped here,' Milly thought about the hole they'd fallen into and the long slide down into the Monster cavern... there was no way to get back out that way.

The lizard went over to Oleander and nuzzled her. Oleander looked up at it and smiled.

'You saved me, didn't you?' She said to the lizard. The lizard seemed to like it when she spoke to it.

'I'm going to call you Lizzy,' Oleander decided.

Dan looked at her as though she was mad.

'You're giving the monster a name?' He gasped.

'I think Lizzy's a nice name,' said Milly.

'You don't even know if it's a boy or a girl,' said Dan grumpily.

'I think she's a girl,' decided Oleander.

'Silly name if it turns out to be a boy,' muttered Dan.

Oleander glared at him, and Lizzy growled.

Dan stood up to avoid Oleander's glare and went to peer into the cave again. Then after a few moments he scanned the ground around his feet and picked up a large rock. He hefted it in his paw, and then threw it into the cave.

Whizz, whizz, clatter, clatter. Two arrows came out of the dark and bounced off the rock as it hit the ground.

'Hmmm,' he said. Then found another rock and heaved that one into the cave as well, landing it on the top of Milly's backpack. This time no arrows came out of the darkness.

'Aha!' He said, turning to Milly and Oleander. 'I think maybe that once an arrow's fired at a particular place in the cave then that's it, no more will fire at the same place.'

Milly thought about that. 'So, if we threw in enough rocks, maybe we could make a path through the cave?'

Dan nodded. 'Just what I was thinking.'

With new hope they all started looking around and finding rocks and bringing them back to the edge of the cave. They soon had a big pile.

'That's enough,' said Dan, and they all stood round the pile to see what Dan planned to do next. He picked up a large rock and threw it.

Whizz! Whizz! Clatter! Clatter!

The rock had landed just short of the backpack and two arrows had hit it. Dan took another rock and threw it to the same place. No arrows came.

'See!' He shouted, delighted.

They all started grabbing rocks and throwing them into the cave. What Dan had guessed seemed to be right. They tried to throw the rocks so they formed a path to Milly's backpack, and then further beyond that to the other side of the cave where the passageway narrowed again. As they threw the rocks, arrows whizzed from everywhere, clattering harmlessly off the rocks onto the cave floor. They soon ran out of rocks and had to go and find more. Finally, there was a path of jumbled rocks that led through the cave. They stopped and looked at it.

'Do you think this will work?' Asked Milly.

Dan took off his backpack and swung it into the cave the same as Milly had. It landed on the path of rocks and no arrows whizzed out of the darkness.

'I'll try it,' Oleander said bravely, and holding up her staff took a first step forward onto the rocky path.

Lizzy squeaked in alarm and jumped in front of her. The lizard pushed her back and then walked out onto the path herself.

'Lizzy!' Oleander cried. But the lizard didn't stop. She walked the whole length of the path without being shot at, then turned round and walked back. She grabbed Milly's backpack on the way and dropped it at her feet.

'Thank you, Lizzy,' said Milly.

'She didn't bring mine back', muttered Dan. Lizzy ignored him.

'Okay, let's go,' said Dan, and set off along the path. They all followed him one by one. Lizzy insisted on going ahead of Oleander, and Milly followed at the back. Dan made it all the way across, having picked up his own backpack as he passed it.

When Oleander was halfway across she stopped and stared at something on the floor of the cave near to the path. It glinted, like some kind of jewel. She crouched down to look at it more closely.

'Don't...' started Milly.

But Oleander was already reaching to pick it up. There was a thin gold chain attached to the jewel, that slowly uncoiled out of the dust on the floor as Oleander pulled it upwards. But then it stuck – like it was caught on something under the dust. Oleander tugged harder and something white appeared.

Oleander gasped and dropped the jewel – the white thing had been a skeleton paw still clutching the chain! The shock made her jump up and a rock underneath her foot moved. Milly reached out to grab her, but that made them both wobble. For a moment Milly thought they could keep their balance, but then they both teetered and fell off the path.

Whizz! Whizz! Whizz! Whizz! Whizz! Five arrows flew out of cracks in the walls of the cave.

Lizzy had seen Oleander bend down and reach out and was already hurrying back. Then she saw Oleander and Milly lose their balance and heard the arrows firing from the dark walls. She launched herself into the air above the mouse queen. She had to save her... but there were five arrows! Maybe she could catch two, possibly three, but not all five. She roared in frustration.

A wash of flames came out of her mouth and incinerated all five arrows in mid-flight. What? That'd never happened before. But then she'd never eaten a fire monster before. She landed on the cave floor beyond Oleander and Milly and stood ready to deal with any more arrows.

Milly lay still where she'd fallen next to Oleander. She'd felt the heat of the flames but didn't know what had happened. She just knew that if she moved she might trigger another arrow.

She heard Dan's voice. 'Oleander, let me grab your paw and pull you up.'

She saw Oleander move next to her.

'Be careful!' She whispered.

There was a loud zing followed by another roar of flames, then Oleander was gone. Dan must've hauled her back onto the path.

What about me? She thought. As if in answer Dan whispered again.

'Milly! You're too heavy for me to pull up, so can you try to get back onto the path on your own?'

She'd have to, she supposed. She rolled sideways to get her paws under her, then paused. No zings from the walls of the cave. Good. Next, she rose until she was standing. Still no zings. All she had to do now was step slowly backwards.

One step... two steps...

Then she saw the jewel which Oleander had been trying to pick up. Could she get it? She took it carefully in one paw and pulled it slowly from the grasp of the bony hand. Then she took a last the step backwards onto the path of stones.

Phew!

She looked around. Oleander was already out of the cave, looking back at Milly with a worried frown. Dan was on the path, heading towards Oleander and beckoning Milly to follow him. And Lizzy... she was standing in the middle of the cave, head darting around, trying to look everywhere at once. It must've been her that had saved them from the arrows!

Milly followed Dan along the path. Every step of the way she expected to hear the zing of another arrow. But none came.

The moment she reached safety Oleander jumped up to hug her. 'Thank goodness you're all right!'

'I'm fine,' Milly disentangled herself. 'And I got this for you.'

Milly handed the jewel to Oleander, and they both took a moment to stare at it. Light sparkled from inside that made Milly gasp. 'What is it?'

Oleander half-smiled. 'I think I might know... but there's no time for it now.' She dropped it into her backpack and looked back into the cave.

'It's all right Lizzy, we're safe,' she called out.

Lizzy looked around and then, instead of jumping back onto the path, started walking across the floor of the cave towards them.

'Careful Lizzy!' Called Oleander.

Arrows whizzed from everywhere out of the darkness. Lizzy jumped and spun and roared and snapped, turning arrows into ash or snapping them in half with her jaws. She seemed very pleased with herself when she finally exited the cave.

'It's a good thing she's our friend,' muttered Dan.

Lizzy looked at him and growled, then went to stand next to Oleander.

🐉 🐉 🐉

They walked on in silence for a while, everyone lost in their own thoughts.

Milly thought about the three challenges. They could easily have been killed by any of them. But now there shouldn't be any more... and so next... next must be the whatever-it-was at the end of the path – the thing that no one was ever meant to see.

She stopped suddenly and said, 'Wait!'

The others looked round at her with tired eyes.

'What?' Asked Dan.

'Aren't we getting near the end of the path now?'

'Maybe... although that page didn't say how long the path was.'

'But, however long it is, won't the next thing we get to be the thing that no one's ever meant to see?'

'What's your point?'

'My point is... suppose we just walk around a corner, and there it is... and we don't realise right away, and we all look at it... and we all get turned into stone, or jelly, or something?'

Oleander groaned. 'You're right, Milly – but what else can we do?'

'Well...', Milly twitched her whiskers, why was she even going to suggest this? 'What if I walk in front, and the rest of you keep back... then if I look at whatever-it-is by mistake, you'll get a warning.'

Everyone went quiet for a few moments, then Oleander nodded. 'Good idea, Milly, but you can't do that, you're the cat of legend... I'll walk out in front.'

'No, Oleander!' Said Dan. 'You're the queen, you can't do it. I'm just an apprentice elder, I'll go in front.'

They couldn't agree and, in the end, Dan huffed in exasperation. 'We can't stand here arguing all day, let's pick stones for it.'

'Pick stones?' Asked Milly.

'We all pick up a small stone and hide it in one paw,'

explained Dan. 'Then we all show which paw we chose and the odd one out loses.'

'Okay...' agreed Oleander unsurely and bent to pick up a stone.

The others did the same and then held their closed paws out in front of them.

'Right,' said Dan. 'Show paws.'

Oleander opened her right paw to show her stone. Milly went next and opened her right paw too. Then Dan opened his left paw.

'Me then,' he said, and immediately took the lead and walked on ahead. As he went Milly saw him drop something from his right paw. Was that another stone? Had Dan cheated to make sure he went in front? Milly decided he was a very brave mouse.

It started to get lighter with each turn of the passageway. Surely that had to mean they were getting near the end. Milly called out to Dan to be careful.

Then up ahead Dan disappeared around a corner and cried out in surprise. Milly froze – was he all right? But then he poked his head back round the corner and laughed.

'It's okay, that page must be wrong,' he called. 'We've just reached the orb!'

12

The Cat of Legend

When Milly caught up with Dan she immediately saw the orb, in a cavern that opened up at the end of a short passageway. It looked about twice her height and was hovering inches above the ground. 'So that's the real orb?'

'Yes,' breathed Dan.

Blues and reds and yellows and every other colour swirled across its rounded surface.

'I don't suppose anyone's been here for hundreds of years,' said Oleander.

Milly thought about the challenges they'd been through and decided Oleander was probably right. Only a mad mouse, or cat, would attempt that path. And only a very lucky one would survive it!

'What I can't understand is why the last part of that page was wrong,' said Oleander. 'When the rest was so accurate. It clearly said that, after the challenges, there would be something that no mouse should ever see.'

Dan shrugged. 'I don't know.'

He started to walk towards the orb.

'Wait!' Shouted Milly. She'd had an idea. When they were running away from the pig monster, Oleander had made her staff flare with bright light. What if the real orb could do the same thing?

'What is it?' Dan asked.

'Suppose this orb can make a sudden bright light like Oleander's did! To blind anyone who comes near.'

'That doesn't seem very likely.'

'But isn't this called the way of the three blind mice?' Questioned Oleander. 'Could that be what it means?'

Dan went quiet for a few moments, then took off his backpack. 'Maybe... and if Milly is right, I actually brought along something that may help.'

He pulled out some strips of cloth. 'I got these in the town – we could use them as blindfolds.'

They all helped each other to tie the cloths around their heads, so that they could easily pull them down to cover their eyes.

'You too, Lizzy,' said Oleander. The Lizard didn't seem to like the idea, but she bent her head down and let Oleander tie the cloth on.

Then they all turned to face the orb.

'What now?' Whispered Milly.

'I think... we pull down our blindfolds... and walk slowly

forwards to see what happens,' replied Dan.

No-one had any better suggestions, so they slid the cloths down over their eyes and started forwards.

Milly kept her two paws stretched out in front of her.

One step... two steps... three steps. What would happen when they reached the orb?

'Is anyone there yet?' Whispered Oleander.

'I can't see a thing,' hissed Dan.

'Grrrrrr,' complained Lizzy.

Milly kept quiet. Had she veered off course? She must've walked twenty paces by now. Maybe she'd walked right past the orb. Then her outstretched paw touched something smooth.

There was a flash of light so bright that it hurt even through the blindfold and her closed eyelids, and then everything went black again. She'd been right! The orb had flashed a very bright light, just like she'd said. It must've been triggered when she touched it... but... where was it now? She felt around with her paws, but there was only empty space. And everything seemed to have gone very quiet.

'Dan... Oleander... where are you?'

No-one answered.

She lifted one corner of her blindfold.

What? Where was she?

She pulled the whole of the cloth off her head and stared around her in wonder.

It seemed like she was outside again, hovering high up in the air. Cloudy sky with patches of blue surrounded her, and below green mountain slopes stretched away to be lost in the depths of a valley. She felt dizzy and fell sideways, and her tummy lurched as for a moment she thought she'd plummet to the ground, but instead she ended up lying on a transparent floor that seemed to curve up around her, as though she was inside a big ball. She looked down and felt sick. The spire of the mouse temple pointed up towards her like a spear, with the temple's battlements spreading out all around it.

In the town below the temple Humble, the captain of the guards, watched the mountain from the high town walls. It was late afternoon and smoke from the mountain had been getting thicker all day. Also, the ground was rumbling more often, and it was worrying him.

Down in the square below, behind the main gates, a crowd had gathered. Humble could hear angry muttering and occasional shouts like 'Why can't they open the gates?', and 'We need to get away,' and 'Who do the guards think they are?'

He could understand that all the mice and cats were afraid. He was afraid. It seemed like the mountain could blow up at any time. But there were rat soldiers down on the bridge, and what would happen if he opened the gates and let everyone rush down there?

He winced as there was a particularly loud bang from the

mountain, and the crowd went silent for a moment as a new gout of black smoke spouted out of the mountain top.

Then the shouting broke out again, even louder, and the gates creaked as everyone pressed forwards against them.

'Stop!' Humble roared down at the crowd but no one took any notice. The shouting and yelling just got louder, and Humble ran along the wall to the tower next to the gates.

'It's no good,' he said to the mouse guards there. 'Get these gates open before someone gets crushed to death.'

The guards started hauling around spokes of a huge wheel, and slowly the bar that locked the gates rose upwards. The crowd noise and pushing and shoving got worse as they realised what was happening, and moments later the gates squealed as they opened, and everyone spilled out onto the road outside.

Humble watched the mice and cats as they ran away down the road outside. He shook his head. He hoped none of them would get hurt when they got to the bridge.

Then something strange happened. A white light flashed and it seemed to Humble that everything looked see-through for an instant. Instead of mice and cats on the road outside he saw skeletons, and the rocks and trees beside the road became transparent so that he could see right through them.

He squeezed his eyes shut and rubbed them with his grubby paws, and when he looked again everything had turned back to normal. Most of the other guards on the walls were rubbing their eyes too, but some of them had turned to stare up into the sky. Humble looked round see what they were looking at and gasped. Above the temple the orb was shining like another sun, and a face had appeared on it, peering down at the mountain and the valley below. The face of a cat.

🐱 🐱 🐱

Deep inside the mountain Dan pulled off his blindfold as the bright light faded. He'd heard Oleander cry out when the light had suddenly flashed. Now he saw she'd taken off her blindfold too and was blinking at him.

'Milly was right,' he said, as he watched Oleander take off Lizzy's blindfold.

'Yes, she was,' Oleander agreed. 'You should apologise to her.'

'Yes... I'm sorry Milly... Milly?' Dan couldn't see her anywhere.

'Where is she?' He muttered.

Then Dan saw the orb had changed. It was no longer swirling with colours, and instead was a shining with a bright white light, and a large cat's face was staring out of it.

'Oh, my goodness!' He breathed.

'Milly!' Squeaked Oleander.

They both stared at the cat's face for a few moments. It looked confused and scared.

'And look at your staff too!' Said Dan.

The orb at the end of Oleander's staff was identical to the

large orb – shining white with Milly's face peering out of it.

Oleander looked from the staff to the orb and back again.

'Is she inside the orb?' She asked.

Dan shrugged then nodded. 'She must be.'

'So, she is the cat from the legend,' Oleander breathed. 'Do you think she'll be all right?'

'I don't know, the carvings of the legend only show the cat's face on the ball, not what happens to her afterwards.'

'Poor Milly, what if she gets trapped in there forever?' Worried Oleander.

'I'm sure she'll be fine,' said Dan hopefully.

Lizzy growled at him.

13

Stopping the Mountain

Milly stared out through the curved walls of the orb. Mostly what she could see was the view of the mountainside. But sometimes she got glimpses of different things. If she sort-of looked a bit sideways a small circle appeared where she could see the faces of Dan and Oleander, and by looking a bit downwards then left or right she saw other circles, showing jerky views of rat soldiers running about, or closeups of big rat's faces, very much like the one from the hallway of columns.

Were those circles views out from the orbs in the elder's staffs?

She focused on Dan and Oleander. Their mouths were moving but everything inside the orb was total silence. She wished she could hear what they were saying, and the instant she had that thought, their voices sounded loud and clear.

First Oleander saying... 'Poor Milly, what if she gets trapped in there forever?'

Then Dan... 'I'm sure she'll be fine.' But he didn't sound very sure.

Could she really be trapped in here? She didn't like that idea.

She looked out at the mountainside again. Then, almost without wanting to, she moved her gaze up to the mountain top. Black smoke was billowing in a tall column that reached into the sky, and deep rumbling sounds suddenly made her tummy quiver. She tore her eyes away – it was too scary – and the rumbling noise was replaced by a sound of distant shouting. Was that from the town? It was out beyond the temple, surrounding by walls with tiny figures on them. If only she could see them better – and, again, as she had that thought her view suddenly zoomed in until she could see mice on those walls in close-up.

She recognized Humble, surrounded by other mouse guards, all staring away from her, down towards the long bridge that crossed the valley.

She focused on listening to what they were saying.

Humble was worrying 'I hope they'll be all right.'

Another mouse replied. 'Those rat soldiers are mean, and they'll be armed with crossbows and swords.'

Who were they talking about?

Milly looked beyond the town and saw more small figures, a whole crowd of them running down the road away from the town.

Humble's voice came again. 'Our job is to look after the town, but we have to help them!'

Then he shouted out to the guards around him. 'We must

leave the walls, and if Mordred attacks then that is our bad luck.'

There was cheering, and Milly saw them all start running, along the walls and then down flights of steps and out of her sight.

Milly gazed further into the distance, towards the bridge that crossed the valley. There were more figures near this end of it, tiny as ants. She zoomed her view in for a moment and saw lines of rat soldiers blocking the entrance to the bridge, with crossbows and swords and lances held ready.

So, that's why the mouse guards were leaving the walls, to go and help the unarmed townsfolk. But even with their help, how would they get past those rats and onto the bridge?

She zoomed her view back out again and movements below caught her attention. In the temple courtyard right underneath her she saw an enormous rat facing three other rats, almost as big as him.

The enormous rat had to be Mordred!

And the rats facing him all had staffs.

What were they saying?

One of the rats sounded very upset. 'What happened to our brother? What have you done to him?'

Mordred came back. 'Me? He decided to go after the cat and the mice on his own. Anyway, he should be fine.'

'Fine? Going up against a cat that's so powerful it's taken over the orb,' said one of the other rats, pointing his staff straight at Milly. 'You should have sent soldiers with him.'

These rats were brothers? And they had another one who was missing? Could he have been the rat that got squished flat by the stone column?

They'd be even more upset if they knew that.

It seemed for a moment that the three rats might attack Mordred. Rat soldiers nearby started pulling out their swords, and a few raised up their crossbows.

Then suddenly a huge explosion sounded from the mountain. Everyone looked up, including Milly from her orb. Fire was billowing from the mountain top now, as well as black smoke, and streams of lava had started flowing down the mountain's sides.

'At last!' Shouted Mordred. 'Nothing can stop the mountain now.'

He waved his paw at the other rats. 'Don't worry about your brother, he is a ninja rat with a staff, nothing can harm him,' Mordred turned away from them and starting shouting orders. 'Everyone get ready, it's time to get out of here!'

As he spoke the mountain began to rumble even louder.

Milly looked around at everything that was going on; the lava flowing faster and faster out of the top of the mountain, the soldier rats dashing around and getting ready to leave, and the mice and cats from the town running down the road to the bridge followed by the town's mouse guards.

This was going to be terrible. Everyone was going to get killed!

Milly turned to the mountain. Dan said that she could stop it. But how? She was inside the orb now... could she make it do something magical? Up on the slopes near the top of the mountain she saw some goats running away from the lava streams. Surely she needed to be closer to the mountain if she was to do anything? And as that thought crossed her mind, the orb started to move. She fell down again as it zoomed away from the temple and over the grass and bushes that climbed the slopes towards the top of the mountain. She staggered back onto her paws as she flew over the poor goats, slipping and skidding as they ran downhill. Then she passed over a huge lava stream before slowing to hover near the plume of black smoke billowing from the very top of the mountain.

Closer! She needed to get closer. The orb moved again, slower now, until through gaps in the billowing smoke she could see right down into a crater in the mountain top. Fire and lava were raging inside.

She had to stop it! But how?

Suddenly a very bad idea came into her head. Very bad indeed.

What if she flew the orb down into that crater? And plunged it right into the lava? Then any magic in the orb would get into the mountain itself, and maybe that would be enough to stop it. She tried as hard as she could to think of something else, but nothing came.

A great gout of flame spat out of the mountain right at her. It splashed off the orb and she didn't even feel any heat.

More and more lava was bubbling up, feeding the flows down the mountain side. Whatever she did, it had to be now! She willed the orb downwards, through the smoke and past the rim of the crater. Would it hurt very much diving into boiling lava? More gouts of fire hit the orb and she could hardly see where it was going.

Down! She thought. Down! Down! Down! And the orb dropped like a stone.

Milly closed her eyes at the last moment.

14

A New Problem

Mordred stared up into the sky in disbelief. The orb had left the temple and was zooming up towards the black smoke coming out of the mountaintop. Surely the mountain couldn't be stopped now?

Around him the rat soldiers were still getting ready to leave, but he continued to stare up at the orb. For a moment it stopped and hovered near the very top of the mountain, then it suddenly plunged downwards and disappeared.

Mordred felt like he'd gone deaf. All the rumbling and exploding noises just stopped. The black smoke coming out of the top of the mountain stopped too, and what was left in the air drifted up and up, until it faded away. The lava flows on the mountainsides became slower until, without any new lava from the mountain top to feed them, they finally halted. Even the sounds of rats running around stopped as they all paused to stare up at the mountain.

No!

Mordred stomped around the temple courtyard in a rage.

This was all Hawthorn's fault. That little mouse had thought he was so clever. 'I can get the mountain to erupt – it'll be the old legend come true – and it'll bury the mouse temple forever'. But not so clever after all! Because he'd ignored the part of the legend that said the mountain could be stopped. Now the temple was not going to be destroyed, and the Weasel was going to be very cross. Mordred's stomping took him over to the main gates of the temple – that were shut tight and locked.

Hmmm... the whole reason for destroying the temple was to stop the mice being able to use it... in particular to stop them using that metal circle inside the Elders' hall to summon their temple mice back from around the world to form an army. But Mordred had control of the temple now and all the mice had been kicked out! Did it need to be destroyed anymore? Or was it enough to just make sure the mice couldn't get back in? Maybe the Weasel would be pleased after all, maybe Mordred had already achieved what the Weasel wanted.

Mordred started thinking hard. He had the temple – but what about those mice in the town? He should clean that out as well. Make sure there were no mice left on this mountain at all. Then he'd feel more secure.

And now might be the perfect time to do that! His scouts had told him everyone had abandoned the town and were running down to the bridge. They would probably turn around and head back to the town now... then close up those gates to make it hard for him to attack them... but for a while they were all stuck out in the open.

'Ninja rats!' He shouted out.

The ninja rat brothers were sulking over by the wall of the courtyard and slinked over to him slowly. The slightly taller of the three stared at Mordred. 'Do you have news of our brother?'

'Don't worry, he'll be fine – but in the meantime I have a job for you,' Mordred gave his best evil smile. 'If you're quick, you can catch everyone from the town while they are still outside. Take all the soldiers here down to the crossroads below the town and cut them off.'

'And what should we do then?'

'Make some use of those staffs of yours,' said Mordred. 'Kill them all!'

The three ninja rats smiled, then turned away and started shouting orders.

Oleander sat silently in the cavern next to the orb. She watched Lizzy wander around looking at the walls and the floor, and Dan stand staring at the orb miserably. What could have happened to Milly? Surely there was something they could do rather than just sit here. Then she suddenly remembered the jewel from the arrow cave – it was still in her backpack! Could that help?

She pulled her backpack towards her and felt inside.

There! She pulled it out by its gold chain.

'Wow!' Dan had been watching her. She glanced up and saw

his eyes were round with surprise.

'Where did you get that?' He whispered, for, moment to be miserable.

'In the arrow cave, it was buried in the dust on the ₊ur.'

'Wow!' Said Dan again.

'There was a horrible skeleton paw holding onto it,' said Oleander. 'That's why I fell over.'

'Can you see anything if you stare into the jewel?' Dan asked.

Oleander put it up to her eye and stared, then immediately jumped back startled.

'Milly!' She cried. 'There's a tiny orb in there, with Milly's face on it, like there is on my staff.'

'I don't believe it,' gasped Dan. 'That's the temple stone.'

Oleander looked at him and nodded. 'The jewel that was lost hundreds of years ago, when the last mouse king disappeared.'

Dan's mouth was hanging open. 'Do you think that skeleton paw belonged to the missing king?'

They both stared at the jewel dangling on the gold chain. There had never been another mouse king, not since the temple stone had been lost.

'The king must have been killed by those arrows', said Dan.

Oleander nodded. 'I wonder why he was trying to get to the orb?'

Dan shook his head slowly. 'We'll never know.'

Oleander held the jewel out towards Dan. 'You should take it. Maybe we can use its power.'

Dan just stared and didn't move, so Oleander reached up and looped the gold chain over his head. The stone nestled against on his chest.

'I feels warm.' He whispered.

'I wonder if that makes you the next mouse king?' Teased Oleander.

'I'm not sure what the elders would think of that idea.'

Milly opened her eyes. Everything seemed very dark. She felt around her and realised she was sitting on the floor of the orb, the walls still curving up and around her. She was alive, then, and still inside the orb. But where was the orb now? She glanced around – light was coming from somewhere. There! Above her. In the circles like windows. She pushed herself back onto her paws so she could peer through them. The first one showed a view of cave walls, lit up by a wavering light, and Dan and Oleander standing close to each other.

'Hello!' Milly called out, but they couldn't hear her.

She tried the other circles. Three were lit more brightly and showed different views of Mordred. He was talking, and Milly concentrated on listening again.

Mordred's voice boomed. 'If you're quick, you can catch everyone from the town while they are still outside. Take our soldiers down now to the crossroads below the town and cut them off.'

Another voice – she couldn't see who it was – and guessed it was one of the rats with a staff. 'And what should we do then?'

'Make some use of those staffs of yours,' said Mordred. 'Kill them all!'

Oh no, thought Milly. Everyone from the town was still in danger! Somehow, she had to help.

She looked back at the circle where Dan and Oleander had just been. There was just a rocky wall now, but that had to be the orb cavern. She needed to get out of this orb now and tell them what was happening. And as she thought that thought, all her fur fluffed up and she felt a rushing, spinning sensation as she was flung through the air.

In the orb cavern Oleander was watching Dan. He seemed different since he'd put on the stone. No longer tired and worried, but full of energy. He paced around the cave.

'We need to do something to help Milly...' he started to say, but then the big orb in the cave suddenly flickered and went black. The same happened to the orb in Oleander's staff.

'Oh no, what's happened?' Breathed Oleander. She couldn't see a thing without the light from the orbs, but then Lizzy helpfully coughed out a small gout of flame.

While the light lasted Dan reached down to get his ghost stick from his backpack. He banged it on the floor so it lit up the cave again with its wavering light.

Dan stared into the big orb hovering in the cave, then down at Oleander's staff.

'They look dead,' he said.

'My staff's never done that before,' said Oleander. 'What about the temple stone?'

Dan held the stone up. 'That looks dead too. And I've only just got it!'

But then a moment later the great orb flickered and then lit up again with swirling colours. The orb in Oleander's staff did the same, and a bight pinpoint of white light flared out of Dan's stone.

Miaow! Milly came flying through the air from the direction of the big orb. They saw her twist and get her paws underneath her so that she landed neatly beside them.

'Milly!' Oleander cried out. 'Are you all right?'

'Yes, I am,' said Milly. 'I think.'

'What happened?' Asked Dan urgently. 'Were you trapped in the orb? How did you get out?'

Milly quickly explained how she'd found herself inside the orb and how she'd used it to stop the eruption.

'Oh, my goodness, you're so brave,' whispered Oleander.

'I knew you could do it,' added Dan.

They all hugged each other. Lizzy came up and nuzzled them too, not wanting to be left out. Milly was happy to be outside the orb again, but knew things were still bad. She told the mice what she'd heard Mordred say about trapping everyone from the town.

'He wants to kill them all?' Gasped Oleander. 'We've got to help them.'

Dan thought for a moment. 'Okay everyone, we must hurry. Get your stuff and then grab my paws.'

In moments they were all holding paws, or in Lizzy's case, scaly talons.

Milly felt everything go weird, and got that sensation of floating, and then suddenly they were outside. She had to take a moment to get her bearings. They were standing at a crossroads where three dry mud roads met; one from above, leading down from the temple, one from the side, coming from the town, and finally one from below, the road up from the bridge. She peered down the bridge-road and saw small dots in the distance, no longer running away but instead heading slowly back up towards the crossroads.

But what about Mordred's rats? She spun around to look up the temple-road, and saw a horde of rats, much closer than the townsfolk, and they were running fast. 'Oh no... they're coming!'

15

A Desperate Plan

Oleander followed Milly's gaze and saw the rats racing down towards them.

Right! She thought. Time to be a real queen.

She stepped in front of the others and held her staff up in front of her. 'I command you to stop!'

Milly was shocked. Oleander's voice had been very loud – had she used magic to do that?

The rats skidded and tumbled trying to stop and finally halted about twenty paces away.

Oleander muttered under her breath. 'I didn't think that would work.'

Dan stepped up next to her and Milly heard him whisper back. 'Me neither.'

A taller rat pushed out in front of the others and walked down towards them slowly. He had an evil grin. 'We have staffs like yours now, mouse queen.'

The rat stopped midway between the rats and the mice and planted the bottom of his staff onto the ground. It swirled with dark reds, and purple crackles of lightning ran up and down its length. The staff hummed, louder and louder, until finally the purple lightning lanced out from the staff, straight at Oleander.

No!

But Oleander twisted her staff to block the lightning and for long seconds the two staffs were connected by greasy purple zigzags. Then Oleander planted her own staff onto the road and lightning turned blinding white and flew back at the rat.

The rat cried out and dropped his staff.

'It takes years to learn to use a staff properly,' said Oleander quietly.

The tall rat bent down and snatched his staff back off the road, then turned and shouted behind him. 'Brothers!'

Two more tall rats, also with staffs, stepped forward to stand next to him.

Three against one! Milly thought that was very unfair. But then Dan moved forwards to stand at Oleander's side, the stone around his neck a brilliant pinpoint of light.

Better... three against two... but Milly still thought they'd need some help. She leaned across to Lizzy to whisper into her ear, hoping she'd understand what she was saying. The lizard nodded once and slowly sidestepped away until she was hidden behind a stand of bushes growing at the roadside.

No-one noticed. They were all staring at the three rats, who were pointing their staffs up at the sky and chanting words Milly didn't understand. A crack of thunder split the air and rain started pouring down, quickly turning into large hailstones that bounced off the ground and clanged as they hit the rat soldiers' armour. A dark cloud formed high in the sky over where the rats stood. The rat brothers moved their staffs to point at Oleander and Dan, and the cloud drifted forwards until in hovered over the two mice.

Two red eyes formed within the cloud, glaring down at Dan and Oleander, and Milly felt her fur prickle until it was standing on end.

'Storm demon!' Shouted the first rat. 'I command you to consume these...'

Milly expected him to continue with, '...mice', or '...mice and that cat,' but he never got that far because half-way through his sentence Lizzy popped out from behind a bush at the side of the road next to him, opened her impossibly large mouth, and gobbled him up with one sharp snap. His staff fell down into a puddle in the middle of the road.

For a moment nothing changed. The other two rat brothers continued staring up at the cloud as Lizzy scuttled back behind the bush again. But then the red eyes turned to stare at the rats, and the cloud tilted and billowed back towards them.

A huge voice boomed. 'Who dares to summon Vortical!'

'Err, our brother did,' said one of the rats.

'And where is he?' The voice boomed back.

The rats looked around desperately.

'...don't know...' the other rat whimpered.

The cloud billowed and a gust of hail hit the rats.

'I am very cross!' Said the cloud.

The two rats cringed. One of them stuttered a reply.

'Erm… we're very sorry.'

His voice was shaking with fear. How had he let his brother talk them into this? I've got a great idea, he'd said. We can summon demons with these staffs, he'd said. Let's get the storm demon to kill everyone from the town, he'd said. But where was he now?

'Did you say "Sorry"?' The cloud seemed to be considering the rat's reply. Seconds ticked by. Then finally the cloud bellowed again, in a voice like a boom of thunder.

'Sorry… is not good enough!'

Black cloudy billows like muscly arms reached down from the cloud and wrapped around the two ninja rats. For a moment all Milly could see was the cloud, and then it swooped up and away into the sky and the ninja rats were gone.

Their two staffs clattered down to join the other one in the puddle.

The rat soldiers, who had been standing back and waiting to see what the ninjas would do to the mice, all gasped at once. It made a very strange sound.

One by one they stepped backwards, then some turned and started running away, and within moments all of them were clanking and clanging their way back up towards the temple as fast as they could go.

Lizzy stepped out onto the road again and Oleander threw herself at the lizard, hugging around her waist. 'Well done Lizzy!'

Dan nodded. 'Yes... good job Lizzy.'

Lizzy burped and this time the puff of smoke that came out was purple.

Then from behind them they heard a ragged cheer and turned to find Humble with his guards and the first of the townsfolk approaching the crossroads.

'How did you manage that?' Humble asked between puffs as he got his breath back, watching the rat soldiers running away up the hill. 'I thought we were all done for.'

'They tried to use magic,' Dan said, but then gestured towards Oleander and Lizzy, who were still hugging. 'But ours was stronger than theirs.'

Humble laughed.

'Well, I'm glad you're on our side,' he said, clapping Dan on the shoulder and nearly knocking him over. He went to join the other mouse guards who were hurrying to get everyone back to the safety of the town.

Dan turned to watch Oleander and Milly fussing over Lizzy, patting her head and saying what a good girl she was. Then he looked up at the retreating rat soldiers, now small dots again, running back to the temple.

So, they'd managed to stop the mountain. And they'd saved everyone from the town. But they'd lost the temple. Mordred and his rats still occupied it, and once they closed its magic gates, it would be hard to get back from them.

They'd need an army to do that. And they didn't have one.

He sat down on the grass, trying to think of what to do next.

'Hmmm...' He said finally and turned his gaze towards the town. It looked like the last of the mice and cats were straggling back through the gates. Could he make them into an army? A small one, at least? He pushed himself up onto his feet and walked over to where the others were now cleaning mud off the three staffs they'd found laying on the road.

'The elders will be glad to get these back,' said Oleander, showing him the staff she'd just cleaned. 'But we only have four of them... I wonder where the last one is?'

Dan shrugged, then he held out his paw. 'Can I look at that one?'

Oleander passed him the staff. 'They seem okay.'

Dan peered at the swirls of colours in the orb at the end of the staff. It reminded him of the big orb that used to float above the temple, the one that Milly had told them she'd flown into the mountaintop. It had been there all his life, and he missed it. He looked up at the temple sadly.

To his surprise the outline of the floating orb had come back and, even as he watched, it seemed that the vague shape in the air was becoming more solid.

'Look at that!' He said.

Oleander looked where he pointed.

'It's coming back,' she said in a delighted voice.

'Hmmm...' Dan repeated. The orb coming back would mean Mordred was safer than ever in the temple, as no one would be able to shift into it.

Unless, he thought, they had a staff. He hefted the staff in his paw, and a plan started to form in his head.

Up in the temple Mordred was stomping around the courtyard again and shouting. He couldn't believe the three ninja rats had been defeated. Who could have done that? He didn't actually miss the ninja rat brothers, as he'd been starting to regret giving them those staffs in any case, but the thought that there was something out there that could so easily defeat them was very worrying. There were disjointed stories coming back from his soldiers about purple and white lightning and a black cloud and some kind of monster lizard, but none of it made any sense.

He glanced around the temple courtyard and walls. He had about a hundred soldiers here, and the gates were locked up tight so no one could get in. But he had a thousand more rat soldiers down on the bridge. He'd feel much safer if they were up here too.

He yelled out. 'Messenger rats!'

He always kept his messengers close by, small wily rats who

could run fast and hide anywhere. In seconds five of them where in front of him, standing up straight and saluting.

'All of you, take different routes down to the bridge and tell the soldiers to pack up their weapons and march up here to the temple – and if you get caught, don't tell those mice anything!'

They nodded and ran towards the gates, and moments later the gates were opened a fraction and they all slipped outside.

Good. Five of them should be enough. At least one should get through to his army.

He hoped.

In the town Dan was looking for Humble. As usual he found him up on the walls keeping a look out for trouble. Humble was a temple mouse, same as all the other town guards, and Dan was hoping there would be enough of them for what he wanted to do.

'There are forty-two of us,' Humble told him when he found him.

Just forty-two? That wouldn't make much of an army. If only there was a way of summoning more temple mice to come back here. Most temple mice spent their time travelling around the world keeping the peace, and when a mouse army was needed they were summoned back using the messaging ring in the temple. He glanced up in the direction of the temple – no chance of doing that at the moment, he thought.

'Are there any more temple mice in the town?' He asked.

Humble scratched his head.

'The students,' he suggested with a pained look.

Dan considered that idea – and decided they'd be more of a liability than a help.

Forty-two would have to do.

'All right, I've got a plan,' he told Humble. 'Can you get your two best guards? And then we'll take them with us to go and see Oleander.'

Oleander, Milly and Lizzy were in the dining room at the Hanging Cat tavern when Dan and Humble found them. Oleander was eating cheese and Milly was chewing her way through another plate of dried fish.

'Hello, is that for me?' Asked Dan, seeing an extra plate had been set out piled high with cheese. He sat down and started nibbling a piece. He was starving!

'Don't mind if we do,' said Humble and, not waiting to be invited, pulled up three extra chairs so that he and two other strong-looking guards could sit down. They all grabbed some cheese from Dan's plate.

'You've met Humble,' said Dan, between bites.

'And these are Berry and Lichen,' he introduced the other two mice who were eating his cheese.

Oleander smiled at them.

Milly wondered why Dan didn't seem to mind everyone pinching his food. She pulled her plate of fish closer to her.

'I have a plan,' started Dan, looking at Oleander. 'But you might not like it.'

He took a long breath then started to explain.

'There are forty-two temple mice guards here in the town,' he said. 'And only a hundred or so rats in the temple. So, if we could get back in, I think we'd have a good chance of defeating them'.

Oleander hated the idea of more fighting. 'You're right, I don't like the sound of it.'

'Well, actually that's not the part I thought you wouldn't like,' Dan said. 'You see, the problem is we don't have enough mice to attack the temple walls from outside.'

'Couldn't you get back in using the tunnels we escaped through?' Suggested Milly.

'It's a possibility,' replied Dan. 'But don't forget the rat soldiers found that passageway, so they'll probably be guarding it.'

'What about shifting in?' Tried Milly.

Oleander shook her head.

'The orb is back over the temple again,' she said. 'It's magic won't let anyone shift in or out.'

'Oh,' said Milly. She'd forgotten about the orb.

But Dan was nodding. 'Milly's on the right track. Shifting is probably our best option.'

Milly felt better, but Oleander looked confused. 'How could we do that?'

'Remember, it's possible to shift in and out of the temple if you have a staff,' Dan explained.

'But only I have a staff,' said Oleander. 'I want to help – but I could never shift forty-two mice up there.'

'I know – but we have three more staffs now,' Dan said. 'And this is the bit of the plan you might not like... I want to lend those staffs to Humble and two of his best guards.'

'But they belong to the elders!' Said Oleander in a shocked voice. 'You can't just lend them to someone else... they won't know how to use them... and what would Ragweed say?'

Milly wasn't good with names, who was Ragweed? Oleander noticed her looking confused.

'Ragweed is the leader of the elders – he was with us in the dungeon,' she reminded Milly.

'Oh, the old, grumpy one?'

'Yes, he can be very grumpy.'

'And about to get grumpier,' put in Dan. 'Because I can't see any other way.'

Oleander sat and thought. Ragweed would be very cross. But she was the queen. She could make this decision and it didn't matter what he said. She started thinking about Dan's plan.

'But even using all the staffs,' she frowned. 'Each of us could only shift three or four mice at a time.'

'Yes, you're right,' agreed Dan. 'But I think I could use the stone.'

Milly saw him touch something hanging round his neck – and wondered what he was talking about.

'And with five of us, we could shift everyone up there just doing two or three trips each,' Dan concluded.

At that point a smallish mouse ran into the room. He slid to a halt, stood to attention, and saluted Humble.

'Mouse reporting!' He said, out of breath.

'Yes?' Said Humble.

'We've found fifteen more temple mice living in the town,' he said. 'They're all coming to the gatehouse as soon as they can.'

'Well done!' Said Humble.

'Great,' said Dan. 'Now we might stand a chance – if we can just get them all into the temple without the rats noticing!'

'But how will we do that?' Worried Oleander. 'We're all going to have to make multiple trips to get everyone up there – won't they spot us before we're finished?'

'That's where Milly comes in,' said Dan.

'Me!' Milly had been happily chewing her fish thinking she wasn't involved in any of this.

'Yes, we need a diversion,' Dan explained to her. 'We need you to keep Mordred and his soldiers distracted while we shift everyone up there.'

'How will I do that?'

'Well, imagine their surprise if you suddenly appeared inside the temple courtyard? The rats have already seen your face on the orb. They'll think you're a great cat magician.'

'Who, me? I can't do any magic!'

'They don't know that. I'll shift you up there, to the front of the courtyard, next to the gates, and then come back before they see me. Then you can get their attention and talk to them for a few minutes. And while they're watching you, we'll shift everyone up in small groups behind their backs!' Dan finished his speech with a big smile, as though it would all be very easy and not dangerous at all.

'And what would I talk to them about?' Asked Milly.

Dan thought for a moment. 'Why not ask them to surrender? You never know, they might even do it.'

'And if they don't?'

'Oh, you'll think of something, you're a very clever cat.'

'Hmmm,' said Milly, not happy at all.

Milly felt Lizzy nuzzle her paw.

'Look,' said Dan, 'Lizzy wants to go with you!'

Lizzy nodded. She really did want to go with her.

Milly looked around, and found everyone was staring at her, like she was their only hope.

Gulp.

She wondered, not for the first time, what was she getting herself into now.

She nodded and they all cheered.

16

The Fight for the Temple

Mordred was up on the temple walls, watching out for signs of his soldiers arriving from the bridge. He paced up and down, even though he should be safe in the temple he was worried. It was still bothering him how the ninja rats had been beaten. Who, or what, could have done that?

Hawthorn watched him pace up and down.

'Don't worry so much,' he said in his sneery voice. 'We're safe in the temple, and once our soldiers get here from the bridge we'll be able to attack and take over the town as well.'

Mordred glared at him. 'They are *my* soldiers, not *ours*.'

Hawthorn swung his staff back and forth in one paw. 'Whatever you say.'

Even though the mouse was only an apprentice elder Mordred knew he was dangerous. Maybe he should have left him locked in the dungeon and not given him that staff. But too late now, and the mouse's magic might still come in useful.

A gasp from the rats down in the courtyard broke the tension between them. Mordred felt a sense of dread. What now? He looked down and saw all the rats were staring at the main gates, and some of them were backing away slowly. Mordred ran to the nearest steps and jumped down into the courtyard in four large leaps. From the bottom he could see what his soldiers were staring at, but he couldn't quite believe it.

The grey fluffy cat was sitting calmly at the other end of the courtyard, just inside of the closed gates, licking one paw and occasionally glancing up to look at the soldiers in front of her. Was she on her own? Mordred glanced around, but he could only see his rats. She was on her own!

'It's the cat,' he heard rats muttering.

'The one from the orb.'

'How did it get in here?'

'What's it going to do?'

'Has it come to eat Mordred?'

That last mutter had come from a rat standing near Mordred.

'Eat me indeed!' He whacked the rat and knocked him over. Ember scurried away before he got hit again.

Mordred glanced back behind him. Had Hawthorn followed? He might his help, in case that cat really was magic. But Hawthorn was nowhere to be seen.

Typical!

He walked over towards the grey cat, while all around him his rat soldiers were backing away.

'Stop, running away you lot... it's just a cat,' he shouted.

But he had to admit he was a bit worried himself. Something

out there had defeated the ninja rats, and this cat's face had appeared on the orb. And now she was here inside the temple. Like she'd shifted here, except that was impossible, at least without a staff. Mordred stopped short at that thought. What if she had one of the missing staffs? He peered at her closely. The cat was still licking one paw and didn't seem to have anything in her other paw.

No. He shook his head to himself. I won't be afraid of a fluffy cat. It's just a cat. A very lucky cat, and quite a brave cat... but just a cat.

Mordred started forwards again and then stopped ten paces away from the cat.

'So, did Dan send you up here to attack me?' Mordred started.

Milly stopped licking her paw and looked at Mordred. 'No, I decided to come up here. I wondered if we could work out a way to avoid any more fighting.'

Was the cat's voice trembling a little?

'Really?' Said Mordred.

'Yes,' she looked around at his rats. 'If you all surrender, we'll let you go unharmed.'

Around the courtyard the rats listened and didn't so much as squeak. They were waiting to hear what Mordred would say to the offer. A day ago, they would have laughed if a cat had asked them to surrender, now they all kept quiet.

Just then a lookout rat scurried down from the gate tower

and ran over to Mordred. He stopped and stared when he saw Milly.

'What?' Mordred asked the rat.

'Our soldiers from the bridge – they're coming. We just saw them reach the crossroads.'

Mordred smiled and looked back a Milly. 'Thank you for your kind offer, cat, but no thank you. Go back the same way you got here, however that was, and tell Dan that I will shortly be coming down to the town to ask for his surrender.'

Mordred waited to see what the cat would do. Silence stretched, and at the same time the smile on Mordred's face stretched too.

'Maybe you can't go back?' Mordred guessed. 'I don't know how you got here, but maybe you're stuck?'

'I can go back anytime I want.'

Yes... the cat's voice was trembling even more.

'Archers!' Shouted Mordred. Up on the walls rats raised their crossbows. Mordred backed away from Milly so he wasn't in the way. Other nearby rats scrambled backwards too.

'Well, you'd better go now, otherwise you're going to end up very dead,' said Mordred, and raised a paw to signal to the soldiers on the walls to fire.

'Wait!' Shouted Milly.

'What now?' Asked Mordred. 'Do you have a last request?'

'Yes – I want you to meet my friend. Her name is Lizzy.'

Something strange stepped out from behind the cat. Green

and gold and scaly.

A lizard? Thought Mordred. The rats who'd run back to the temple had mentioned a monster lizard. But this thing was only about the same size as the cat, nothing to be scared of. He slashed his paw down. 'Fire!'

There were forty-seven rats on the walls with crossbows, and forty-seven arrows zinged towards Milly and Lizzy. The rats trained a lot and were good shots, and every one of them was on target. But before the arrows reached them Lizzy roared out a gout of flame, tinged with purple and green.

Forty-six arrows turned to ash in the air. The forty seventh arrow was a bit too fast, and Lizzy jumped up and caught it in her jaws instead.

The smoke cleared and Milly saw Mordred and his soldiers still in the courtyard, their fur a bit singed and looking shocked. Lizzy crunched and the two halves of the arrow in her mouth fell onto the ground at her feet.

At the other end of the courtyard, the air shimmered and Oleander appeared with four temple mice from the town. It was the fifth time she'd shifted up to the temple, and she was feeling faint from the effort.

Humble, Berry and Lichen, the other mice with the staffs, had done their best but had only managed two shifts each.

However, Oleander and Dan had done extra shifts and they'd managed to get all forty-two temple mice guards, and also the other fifteen temple mouse volunteers, safely up into the temple. Everything had gone according to Dan's plan. Only a couple of rat soldiers had noticed when one of the groups of temple mice had arrived, and they'd been quickly captured and tied up.

The temple mice had disguised themselves in big cloaks as each group of them arrived and then spread out amongst the rats, some going up onto the walls, some edging around the sides of the courtyard. All the rats had been so intent on watching Milly and Mordred that, so far, they'd gone completely unnoticed.

Dan had been waiting for Oleander's last shift. He threw some dark cloaks to the four mice with her and told them to climb some nearby steps up onto the walls. Then he whispered to Oleander. 'Now you must get out of here, shift back to the town where you'll be safe.'

Oleander was indignant. 'No, I can fight as well!'

'But you are the queen, who will lead the temple mice if something happens to you?' Dan said urgently.

Oleander was torn. She wanted to fight, but she understood that Dan was right.

'All right,' she said after a moment.

She closed her eyes, visualised the side of the road outside the hanging cat tavern, then tried to shift.

'Oh', she said, when she opened her eyes and found she was still in the courtyard.

'What is it?' Asked Dan.

'I can't shift, something's wrong.'

'You look exhausted. Maybe you just need a rest.' Dan looked around, if Oleander couldn't shift, he needed to hide her. The doors to the inside of the temple stood open behind them. They led into a short passageway, that in turn led to a great hall. Dan already knew that either side of that short passageway were two small rooms. The rat soldiers they'd tied up had been hidden in one of them. But Oleander could hide in the other one! He led her there quickly and pushed the door open to check inside. It was a square stone room with a large table with chairs around it. At the back there was a small archway and, under its shadows, a winding stone staircase led up into darkness. He beckoned to Oleander. 'Just say in here and shift away as soon as you can manage it.'

'Okay,' Oleander suddenly hugged him. 'But you be careful.'

Dan didn't know what to do, a queen had never hugged him before. But they had been through a lot together, so he hugged her back.

'I will,' he nudged her into the room and closed the door behind her, wishing he had a key to lock it.

🐀 🐀 🐀

Dan got back to the courtyard as the purple greenish smoke

from Lizzy's flames finally cleared. Everyone in the square had gone quiet. It seemed that none of them dared to move.

Then above Dan, up on the walls, there was a bang, and white light glared out. Dan walked further into the courtyard so he could look up at what was happening.

Hawthorn was up on the walls! With his staff planted on the stones by his feet, and white swirls and crackles circling his head.

Somehow the other apprentice must have escaped – and managed to get hold of the final missing staff from somewhere. Now the rats had no chance!

The white swirls and crackles around Hawthorn twisted into an odd globe shape which arced into the air, then wobbled like a huge soap bubble down into the courtyard and towards the gates. Yes! Hawthorn was going to use it on Mordred! But it sailed past the huge rat and headed straight for Milly and Lizzy. A moment later it hit them.

'Oh no!' Muttered Dan.

The globe didn't explode or seem to hurt them at all. Instead, it caught them inside it.

The rats in the courtyard and on the walls cheered, seeing the scary cat and her lizard trapped.

Dan was shocked. Why would Hawthorn do that? Had he made a mistake? Then Dan heard Mordred shout out.

'Well done Hawthorn... hold them there while I finish them off!'

Mordred grabbed a long spear from a nearby rat and ran towards the crackling globe.

In one huge rush, Dan realised the truth. Hawthorn wasn't on their side. Maybe he never had been. It all made sense; that trip to see the Weasel, how Hawthorn had got past the rats back at the river, and how he'd escaped again here and managed to get one of the elder's staffs.

Dan couldn't allow Milly to be hurt. He put his paw to his mouth and let out a piercing whistle, which was the signal to the temple mice to attack, and at the same time pulled out his sword and threw it with all his strength at Hawthorn up on the walls.

He missed. The sword sparked on the stone next to Hawthorn's feet and clattered away harmlessly. But it scared the skinny mouse enough that he jumped back out of sight with a frightened squeak. The white light and crackles from his staff blinked out of existence.

Dan twitched his nose grimly. He would deal with Hawthorn later, but now he needed to go and help Milly. He turned and ran through the middle of the courtyard, dodging and weaving between knots of fighting temple mice and rats.

Milly and Lizzy were shocked to find themselves suddenly enclosed by a globe of white swirls and crackles. Lizzy opened her mouth to roar but Milly stopped her. Suppose her fire couldn't get out of the globe and just incinerated them instead?

She tried touching the crackling wall of the globe and jumped back as it stung her paw.

Through the swirls she saw Mordred running towards them with a long spear.

'Look out!' She shouted, pulling Lizzy down with her as she ducked.

The spear came straight through the globe walls and went over their heads. Mordred pulled it back out, laughing. He could just keep stabbing through the globe until he speared them!

Then a loud whistle sounded and shouting broke out.

Mordred hesitated for a moment, looking all around him. Mice had appeared from everywhere and started fighting the rats. He turned back and glared at Milly. 'So cat, it was all a trick, you came here to distract me.'

He raised the spear above his head and aimed another almighty jab at her. 'But it's the last trick you'll ever play.'

Fizz, crackle, pop!

The globe made a weird noise and disappeared.

Lizzy jumped forwards and snapped Mordred's spear in her jaws before it could hit Milly. She jerked her head to haul it out of Mordred's grasp, then snapped it in two and tossed it aside.

Milly had never seen Mordred look scared before, but he looked it now. As Lizzy opened her mouth to snap at him again, he was already twisting round and his paws were scrabbling the ground to get away.

Snap!

'Youch!'

Lizzy had nipped the tip of his tail, which must've have really hurt, because it made him run even faster. He hurtled away across the courtyard, bashing aside fighting rats and mice, with Lizzy chasing after him and snapping her jaws.

'Lizzy!' Milly called, worried the lizard could get hurt. But it was no good, Lizzy had already disappeared into the crowd of rats and mice and the clouds of dust they were kicking up as they fought.

🐊 🐊 🐊

The fight between the temple mice and the rats raged in the courtyard and up on the walls that surrounded it. The temple mice were outnumbered by the rats, who were also bigger and stronger. And worse, the rats had armour of metal or chain mail, while the mice only had their belts of weapons to cover their fur. But they were temple mice and even though they couldn't shift in the temple – which was one of their favourite fighting tricks – they were still faster and better fighters than the rats.

Dan finally made it to the gates and was shocked to find Milly on her own without Lizzy to protect her. Milly told him how the lizard had run off chasing Mordred.

'You're not a soldier, Milly – I'll stay and protect you,' panted Dan.

As he said that Milly pounced past him and swiped with her paw at a rat that had been about to stab Dan with his sword – the rat flew through the air and hit the temple wall, then slid down it unconscious.

'Or maybe you could protect me,' said Dan, as he grabbed up the sword that the rat had dropped.

At the other side of the courtyard five mice were backed up against the side wall facing ten rats with long spears. The rats held metal nets that snared the mouse's swords whenever they tried to dart forward to attack between the spears. One mouse tripped and fell – and a spear through one leg pinned him to the ground. Another mouse jumped forward and slashed at the spear – but a net whistled over his head and trapped his arms.

'Forward!' The rats with the spears saw their chance to finish off the five mice and lunged forwards.

'Arrgh!' Came a shout from above, and a brown shape dropped from the walls onto the rats.

Humble landed amongst the rats and knocked three of them over, then started slashing at the rest with his sword. Three more rats fell before they knew what was happening, and then the trapped mice took their chance and rushed to help Humble, slashing with their own swords.

'Thank you, sir!' Gasped the mouse who'd been caught in the net as he pulled himself free.

'Help me with him!' Humble shouted back, and they both grabbed hold of the mouse who'd been injured by the spear and dragged him to the side of the courtyard.

🐑 🐑 🐑

Dan and Milly were fighting well as a team. Waves of rats had tried to attack them but had either been flung away by Milly or wounded by Dan's whirling sword. Then Dan felt the whizz of an arrow past his ear. Arrows! He looked up around the walls. There! A group of rats with crossbows, constantly reloading and shooting down into the crowd below – not seeming to care who they hit. He concentrated briefly on the space behind them and the stone around his neck shone brightly as he shifted up onto the walls. He caught them completely by surprise.

'Look out!' One shouted – but then squealed as Dan thrust his sword at him and caught him in the shoulder. In seconds four of the rats were down clutching at wounds and the rest were backing away from Dan. Two fired their crossbows in a panic but their arrows flew high over Dan's head – three others were trying to reload as they scrambled backwards. They all forgot about the edge of the wall and the drop down into the courtyard and, with howls of dismay, they fell down into the battle raging below.

Dan rushed to the edge and looked down – stupid rats. But then he saw a huge fat rat waddling towards the unmistakable figure of Humble. Humble and another mouse were dragging an injured mouse away from the fighting and didn't see the big rat coming. The rat raised a huge hammer over his head to smash down on Humble. Dan grabbed a metal disk with starlike spikes from one of his belts and threw it. The disk sizzled through the air and hit the fat rat in its broad back. The spikes must have gone through the rat's chain mail because it gasped in pain.

Humble heard and spun round just in time to dodge the huge hammer. It came down on the poor injured mouse instead who screamed as it hit his other leg. Humble roared in anger and slashed his sword with terrible force at the fat rat, tearing the chain mail across its chest and sending it staggering back. It dropped its hammer and ran – with the much quicker Humble chasing it across the courtyard between the other fighting rats and mice.

Berry and Lichen kept together. They'd promised to look after their staffs, but they'd turned out to be as much a liability as a help. They had to hold them with one paw while using their other paw to swing their swords – but at least the staffs allowed them to shift.

They suddenly found themselves on their own as a large knot of rats rushed across the courtyard towards them.

'Shift!' Gasped Lichen.

They disappeared – astonishing the rats who found

themselves slashing their swords at thin air rather than temple mice.

They reappeared next to the wall on the opposite side of the courtyard, just as a whole group of rats fell from the wall above and nearly landed on top of them. Next to the rats landed a clatter of crossbows. Lichen glanced upwards and saw Dan looking down.

'Grab those crossbows and get up here!' Dan shouted.

Lichen and Berry scooped up all the crossbows and quivers of arrows, then shifted up onto the walls next to Dan.

'Good mice!' Dan breathed. 'Now let's give the rats a taste of their own medicine.'

The mice grabbed a crossbow each and started firing arrows down into the courtyard below. Temple mice are expert shots, and more and more rats starting falling to their own arrows.

The fighting began to die down as the mice started to outnumber the rats who could still fight. All over the courtyard the remaining rats backed up against the walls, tired and overwhelmed by fighting skills of the mice.

'Stop!' Dan's shout echoed across the courtyard. He still had a crossbow up on the wall and was holding it ready to fire.

It took a few moments, but everyone did stop. The groups of mice and rats faced each other in a tense silence, glancing up at Dan then back down warily in case the fighting started again.

'Surrender now and no one else will be hurt!' Dan shouted.

Dan could see the rats glancing around uncertainly. They were looking for Mordred – waiting for orders. But he was nowhere to be seen. In ones and twos at first, then all in a rush, the rats threw down their weapons and put their paws in the air.

🐀 🐀 🐀

From the room just inside the temple Oleander listened to the sound of fighting out in the courtyard. She was sitting on one of the chairs trying to decide what to do. She'd tried shifting several times, but still couldn't manage it. She felt helpless, she couldn't get away from here and she couldn't help with the fighting either.

There was a crash and a bang outside the door followed by running footsteps. She looked at it in alarm, but nothing came through. Seconds later more footsteps sounded, disappearing in the same direction as the first ones.

She went and put her ear to the door, and heard clangs of metal and shouts and screams. That had to be coming from the fight in the courtyard. Would Dan be okay? And what about Milly and Lizzy? She yearned to be out there helping. She reached for the doorhandle and started to turn it.

'Well, well, what do we have here?' A sneering voice came from behind her.

She spun around and there at the bottom of the spiral of stone stairs at the back of the room was Hawthorn!

'Hawthorn, you're all right!' Oleander gasped. How had he escaped from the dungeons? Then she saw he had a staff, and knew immediately it was the missing one, the staff of conquest. 'How did you get that staff back from the rats?'

She never thought Hawthorn would've had it in him to take on a rat – let alone one with a staff.

Hawthorn looked at the staff in his paw thoughtfully. 'Yes... I did get it from a rat... he didn't really know how to use it.'

Oleander was sure it was an exciting story, but she didn't have time to hear it now. Hawthorn had been an apprentice elder for ten years – she didn't like him much, but she knew he was good with magic. With the two staffs they could really make a difference in the battle outside.

'Quickly, we must go and help!' She said, pulling open the door.

'No! Wait, your majesty,' Hawthorn said.

She looked back at him impatiently, the skinny rat suddenly looked panicky. 'What?'

'This staff. There's something wrong with it,' he said.

Oleander closed the door again and went over to him. 'It looks all right, doesn't it work?'

'The rat I got it from... he may have damaged it. It's been losing power, and now it won't do anything at all,' Hawthorn said. 'I think it needs re-setting.'

'Re-setting?' Asked Oleander, she'd never heard of such a thing. 'How do you do that?'

'Ragweed showed me how to do it,' Hawthorn explained. 'It can be done using another staff.'

'Oh, I see', she planted her staff on the flagstones in front of her. 'All right, I can use mine, what do I need to do?'

'Well, you don't need to do anything,' said Hawthorn sweetly. 'Just lend me your staff for a moment and I will be able do it'.

Hawthorn held out his paw.

Lend him her staff? After losing it once already, Oleander wasn't sure she wanted to let go of it.

'Come on, you can trust me,' said Hawthorn.

'Well, of course I can trust you,' said Oleander, and reluctantly held out her staff to him.

'Thank you,' said Hawthorn and, as he took it from her, a nasty smile crept onto his face.

17

Saving the Mouse Queen

The temple mice were collecting the weapons dropped by the rats and tying them up. Dan watched nervously. Everything seemed to be going to plan, but there was still no sign of Mordred or Hawthorn. Humble came down the steps from the top of the wall to stand next to Dan. He leaned over to whisper in Dan's ear.

'I don't want to worry you,' he said. 'But there are about a thousand rats outside.'

A thousand! Thought Dan. They could beat a hundred – but not a thousand.

'Thank goodness they can't get in,' he said.

The magical gates were very strong. But then he remembered his missing key – Mordred must still have that. And Hawthorn had his own key as well. What if one of them got to the gates? They could open them easily.

'We need to stop anyone getting near to the gates and unlocking them! From inside or outside.' He said urgently to Humble.

Humble nodded.

'Yes, sir! I'll put a squad on the ground this side and put archers up on the walls to fire down at anyone outside,' he ran away, waving mice towards the gates.

Dan watched him go. He was surprised Humble had called him 'sir'. He'd never done that before.

As he was wondering about that, an unnaturally loud voice suddenly boomed across the courtyard.

'Em, please can I have your attention?'

That whiny voice... Dan knew it only too well. It was Hawthorn. He spun around to work out where it was coming from.

Hawthorn was coming through the double doors from inside the temple – with Oleander just in front of him. Everyone had stopped to look, he must've used magic to make his voice so loud.

Oleander had a rope tied around her waist and Hawthorn was holding the other end. She looked scared, and she didn't have her staff. Hawthorn was pointing his staff at her back, and it was crackling with sparks up and down its length.

He prodded the queen to keep her walking forwards, and as the staff touched her, she jumped and cried out.

'As you can see, I have your queen,' Hawthorn's loud voice said.

'She's your queen too!' Shouted Dan. He couldn't believe Hawthorn was threatening poor Oleander.

'No, I think not,' said Hawthorn. 'Not anymore, anyway, eh Oleander?' He prodded her again and she yelped. Temple mice all around the courtyard raised their weapons.

Hawthorn stopped walking and jerked the rope to stop Oleander too.

'What are you doing?' Shouted Dan.

'Well, I believe my rat soldiers are outside. And we need to let them in,' said Hawthorn.

'Your soldiers? Don't they belong to Mordred?'

Dan started walking as he spoke. If he could get closer he might be able to help Oleander.

'Well, Mordred's not around, but if he does turn up, I'm sure he won't mind me giving them orders,' said Hawthorn.

Up on the wall mice raised loaded crossbows. Dan hoped none of them tried firing – they could hit Oleander.

'Don't worry about me!' Oleander called out bravely, as though she'd read his thoughts. 'Don't let him open the gates.'

Hawthorn glanced up at the walls.

'It feels a bit too dangerous out here,' he muttered. He started to back away towards the temple doors again, pulling the rope so that Oleander had to walk backwards with him.

'Maybe I'll wait back here,' he called out. 'And let you go and open the gates for me'.

'I don't have a key anymore,' Dan said, keeping pace with Hawthorn as he edged backwards. Hawthorn stopped when he was inside the temple doorway again and shielded from the crossbows.

'Oh yes, you lost it, didn't you,' he sneered. 'And let all these nasty rats into the temple... but don't worry, Dandelion, you can use my key instead.'

'No, don't do it, Dan,' shouted Oleander.

'I can't let him hurt you,' Dan hissed, still edging forwards.

Hawthorn watched Dan closely. He knew the other mouse could easily beat him in a fight. But he was sure Dan was no match for him magically – especially now he had the staff.

The other mouse was getting close now. Too close!

'Stop right there,' he fumbled to open a pouch in his belt, then pulled out a small golden key. Then he threw it towards Dan. 'There, now pick it up and do as I say, or your queen will get frazzled.'

Oleander let out a sob as Dan picked up the key. 'Don't do it, Dan.'

How brave, thought Hawthorn sarcastically, as he watched Dan bend down and pick up the key, then turn away and head back towards the temple gates.

Yes!

He relaxed. He was safe now. He watched Dan continue out into the sunlight of the courtyard and start winding his way between shocked temple mice and tied up rats towards the outer gates of the temple.

'Why are you doing this, Hawthorn?' Oleander wailed.

'It's no concern of yours,' Hawthorn snapped. 'After today I will be in charge here'.

'You want to run the temple?'

'Not just the temple... everything, the world...'

Oleander was shocked. 'Why would you want that?'

She really meant what she asked him. She was the queen, but not by choice. It had been bad enough being a Princess, but then her mother had disappeared on a trip to find new healing herbs, and she'd been crowned the new queen. She'd barely finished school. She would much rather just be a normal mouse.

'I will do a better job,' said Hawthorn. 'The mice will be made great again!'

His voice was bitter, and he glared at Oleander. His words stung her, maybe because there was some truth in them. She knew she wasn't doing the job of a proper queen.

She stared at her feet. If she ever got out of all this, she was going to have to make some big decisions. She couldn't keep hiding up here in the mouse temple. She would have to go back to her throne in Mouse City.

Hawthorn realised he'd been distracted and glanced back at the courtyard. Where was Dan? He should've reached the gates by now, but there was no sign of him anywhere.

Then suddenly something shoved him from from behind,

and the floor came up to hit him in the face. He kept one paw clutched around his staff, he had to keep hold of that, but he dropped the rope that held Oleander.

He rolled sideways and staggered back onto his feet, but by then Oleander had escaped and Dan was standing in front of her.

'Dandelion! How did you get back here?'

The annoying young apprentice just smiled and folded his arms.

Hawthorn steadied himself, then raised his staff. 'No matter, you're no use to me now!'

His staff sparked into white fire, and Hawthorn noticed Dan glance back to make sure Oleander was behind him. Hawthorn laughed. 'How noble... but you can't protect her.'

Hawthorn's white fire was tinged with black as it flashed out from his staff straight at Dan's heart.

Dan cringed. But as the fire hit him the stone around his neck flared with bright light and sucked Hawthorn's fire into it

'What?' Hawthorn was staring at the stone around Dan's neck. 'What's that you're wearing? It's not, is it? Not the temple stone?'

Dan nodded.

'But where did you find it? It's been lost from memory since the old king disappeared.'

Dan shrugged. 'Does it matter?'

'Matter?' Hawthorn screamed. 'That an apprentice is running around with the most powerful gem in the world around his neck. A gem that should be worn by someone who knows how to use it.'

Hawthorn pointed his staff at the roof and shot out a rocket of fire. A great crack sounded and stones from the ceiling started raining down. Dan jumped backwards, pulling Oleander with him. Was Hawthorn trying to kill them all?

After a few moments the crashing stopped and dust swirled in the air. Dan peered to see through it, ready for any further attacks. But once it started to clear he realised the skinny mouse was gone.

Hawthorn had escaped!

18

Return of the Rats

Mordred was a fast runner, particularly with a monster chasing after him. After crashing past the fighting rats and mice in the courtyard he ran through the open doors at the far end of the courtyard and into the temple. He clattered along a short passageway then into the great hall, skittering and sliding as he crossed the worn flagstones to get to the maze of corridors beyond.

He knew where he was going. He had a plan to escape the monster. But he needed to be far enough ahead of it, or the plan wouldn't work. He reached another big hallway with a wide flight of stairs leading up to the next floor. He bounded up the stairs with no hesitation and glanced back when he reached the top. The monster skidded into the hallway below him and paused to roar flames in his direction.

Mordred ducked down and ran away down another corridor. The monster was still too close! He needed something to distract it or slow it down. And as he thought that thought, he turned into a new corridor and came face to face with a shocked little rat.

Ember was happy. He finally had a safe job to do.

His Sergeant had told him to guard a corridor in the middle of the temple. There was meant to be a secret passage somewhere nearby and Ember had to keep watch in case any mice tried to use it to get in.

To start with he'd been nervous. But as hour after hour ticked by it had begun to seem very unlikely that the mice were going to try to get in this way. There were chairs at the side of the corridor that looked very inviting. He'd decided it wouldn't matter if he had a bit of a sit down – or even rested his eyes for a while.

He'd just been just dozing off when a clatter of pawsteps had made him jump up in alarm.

Mice! He thought in a panic. But then he realised the sound was coming from the wrong way. He stood uncertainly, not sure what to do. And then suddenly Mordred himself skidded around the corner! He seemed in a terrible hurry and snapped at Ember when he saw him.

'I've got a job for you!'

Ember hated those words.

'There's something following me – you have to stop it if it tries to get past.'

Mordred hardly paused as he shouted orders at the shocked little rat in the corridor. Then he continued down the corridor and skidded around into a dark side-passage. This had to be the right one! He had no time to get it wrong. There... that blank stretch of wall! He pressed at the bricks at chest-level until one moved and, with a soft grinding noise, a square of wall opened up to reveal a tunnel. Thank badness! He jumped into the tunnel and then pushed the wall back into place behind him. Then he leaned against it trying to breathe quietly.

'Aha! Stop right there!' He heard the voice of the small rat shout from outside.

Then there were some crashes and bangs. Then silence. Then Mordred heard clicking steps just the other side of the wall he was leaning against. That must be the lizard! No way that small rat could've done much more than slow it down. Seconds ticked by slowly. Until finally there was a huff of frustration and the sound of the clicking footsteps walking away.

Mordred slid down the wall and sat down. That was close... he concentrated on getting his breath back and trying to think. He was in the secret tunnel that those annoying mice and their cat had used yesterday to escape from the temple. His rats had reported the trick of getting over the lava, and he was sure the tunnel must come out somewhere between the temple and the town.

This was how he was going to get away!

And once he had got away... he was going to take his army

and make a run for it back across the bridge. He'd had enough of the Weasel and his crazy plans.

It didn't take Mordred long to get to the end of the tunnel. The lava steps had been easy – he didn't know why his rats hadn't chased the mice across them. He was in a good mood as he burst out into the daylight again on the hillside.

'Mordred!' A familiar voice said. 'How nice to see you.'

Mordred jumped. It was the Weasel. The last voice he wanted to hear. How had he guessed where Mordred would be?

'Things are not going exactly to plan,' the Weasel said, glaring at him. 'The mountain seems to have stopped erupting.'

'Hawthorn let us down,' said Mordred, not wanting to take any of the blame.

'Yes, he is a silly little mouse,' said the Weasel. 'But you… the great rat commander… have also allowed the mice to take back their temple.'

Mordred was cross. But he was too scared of the Weasel to show it. 'They took us by surprise.'

'Hmmm. Well, next time you need to be more careful.'

'Next time?'

'Yes, Mordred. You still have your army here. So all is not yet lost.'

Mordred's heart sank. So much for his plan to run away.

'Yes, the Weasel continued. 'Your whole army, I believe.

Bringing that was very good thinking. Because now you can use it to lay siege to the temple and take it back from the mice again.'

Mordred nodded. 'Yes... that was my plan... of course.'

What else would it have been?

'Good – because I really don't want to be let down again today.'

The Weasel smiled – then disappeared.

Dan and Oleander walked out of the temple into the courtyard holding paws. Dan worried whether he really should be holding paws with a queen, but she had insisted.

Humble ran up to them.

'What happened, are you all right?' He asked, his words tripping over each other.

Oleander smiled. 'Yes, thanks to Dan.' She glanced sideways at him and he felt awkward.

'Queen Oleander was very brave,' he muttered.

'I am sure she was,' agreed Humble. 'But what about that Hawthorn, never did like him. Did you catch him?'

Dan shook his head. 'No, he shifted away. He's gone.'

'Not far, I bet, and he's still got that key of his. I'll warn the guards to watch out for him in case he shifts back with that staff and tries to open the gates.'

Humble was about to rush off and shout more orders, but Dan stopped him by holding up a golden key. 'No need to worry about that, I got his key.'

Humble shook his head in wonder. 'You are a clever mouse. No doubt about that.'

'Yes, he is,' agreed Oleander, and Dan felt her squeezing his paw.

'Don't forget about Mordred though, he still has my old key,' Dan reminded Humble. 'And we don't know where he is.'

Milly was listening to their conversation and sighed – she was fed up with all this talk about keys. 'Why can't someone just change the lock?'

She found everyone looking at her in surprise, when she'd expected them to all laugh and say it was impossible.

'I never thought of that,' muttered Humble. 'Can we do it?'

Dan looked at Oleander. 'I think we can – can't we?'

Oleander nodded slowly. 'Yes. It's a magic lock. Why didn't we think of it before?'

'How do we do it?' Dan asked.

'Well, all the five staffs must be present, and then it's a simple spell,' she replied.

'Five staffs? That's a shame,' said Dan, wishing he'd been able to stop Hawthorn getting away with the staff of conquest. But Oleander was squeezing his paw in excitement. 'It might work with just four staffs plus the temple stone!' She pulled him towards the gates. 'Come on, let's try it.'

Humble grabbed a passing mouse and told her to find Berry

and Lichen, the other mice with the staffs, and send them to the gates. Then he hurried to catch up with Dan where he was being pulled along by Oleander.

Berry and Lichen came running up just as they reached the gates.

'Okay, now all stand in a circle right here,' said Oleander. She positioned them next to the door. Milly watched from the side and saw Oleander reach out her staff to touch the lock. Gold light flowed down her staff and then rippled across the other staffs and finally Dan's stone. Oleander muttered some words that Milly couldn't make out, and then there was a tinkle of metal and six new golden keys fell onto the ground out of nowhere.

'We normally have a nice cushion for them to fall onto,' explained Oleander as she bent down to pick them up and dust them off.

'So the lock's changed now?' Asked Milly. Was it really that easy?

'Yeah... I suppose,' replied Dan. Then he reached into a pouch and pulled out the old key he got from Hawthorn.

What would happen to that now?

'Ouch,' breathed Dan, and dropped the key onto the ground.

Milly watched it fall into the dust, then gasped as she saw it start to melt. In seconds it was just an expensive puddle on the ground.

Suddenly there was a roar of rats shouting from outside.

'The rats are attacking!' A voice called from the walls above the gate.

Immediately there were thwangs of crossbows as mice up on the wall started firing. Oleander handed Dan one of the new keys and put the rest away into a pouch on her belt. Then she led the way up the nearest steps onto the wall to see what was happening. Milly caught up with them and was amazed when she peeped over the battlements. Outside, a horde of rat soldiers were watching from just out of arrow range, and closer something like a huge tortoise was edging towards the gates.

Humble rumbled next to her. 'That's a squad of rats holding shields over their heads so we can't get them.'

Either side of Milly, mice were firing their crossbows, but the rats with the shields kept coming in their tortoise formation. As they got closer it started to look more like a hedgehog, there were so many arrows sticking out of the shields.

'I bet Mordred's under there somewhere,' said Dan from Milly's other side. 'And that he's going to try to use my old key to get in.'

Humble gave him a worried glance. 'Are you sure the lock's been changed?'

Dan nodded. But Milly noticed that behind his back he'd crossed his fingers.

'What I can't work out is, why hasn't my old key melted like Hawthorn's did,' Dan muttered.

'Maybe they don't all melt at the same time?' Suggested

Oleander from behind him.

Milly had a different thought. 'Or maybe they only melt when you get them out to use them. Otherwise, they'd be dangerous, they could just suddenly melt in your pocket.'

Dan glanced sideways at her. 'Clever cat,' he murmured. 'You could be right.'

A sudden shout came from under the rat shields – like a large rat in pain. 'What...no... ouch... arrghh!'

Milly smiled. It sounded like she was right.

Then the voice shouted again. 'Back! Back! We'll just have to do this the hard way.'

The hedgehog of shields edged away again to rejoin the rest of the rat army.

'He's not giving up by the sound of it,' Humble muttered.

'No,' agreed Dan. 'This isn't over yet.'

Milly sat in the courtyard leaning back against one of the walls. The rats didn't seem to be able to get into the temple. But they weren't showing any signs of giving up and going away either. Oleander and Dan were sitting nearby. They'd all spent ages talking about how they might get rid of the rats, but so far no one had come up with anything that had much chance of working. Now they were all sitting quietly, lost in their own thoughts.

Nearby Lizzy was wondering around the courtyard, peering

into cracks in walls and behind boxes and pillars.

'He's still looking for Mordred,' said Milly. 'Doesn't he know he's outside now?'

Dan looked over at the lizard. 'Do you think if we just let Lizzy out of the gates that he'd go and find Mordred and chase him away?'

Oleander squeaked. 'There's a thousand rats out there. Even Lizzy can't fight that many!'

'Yes. Poor Lizzy might get killed,' added Milly.

Silence descended again, the same as before, except now Oleander kept looking up and glaring at Dan.

Four mice edged up to them and coughed to get Oleander's attention. She looked up. 'Oh, hello.'

Milly recognized them, they were the elders from back in that smelly dungeon. Ragweed, Chestnut, Damson and Acorn. Someone must've gone down and let them out.

'We heard about Hawthorn,' Ragweed said. 'Terrible... our own apprentice – none of us guessed he'd turned against us.'

'No,' said Chestnut. 'None of us.'

'And we're all loyal,' added Acorn.

'Good,' said Oleander.

'The thing is, err, has anyone seen our staffs anywhere about?' Ragweed asked.

Oleander shook her head sadly.

'I'm really sorry Ragweed, but your staff was stolen by Hawthorn, and we don't know where he is.'

Ragweed looked devastated. The old mouse shook his head and wondered away across the courtyard. They all watched him go.

'What about our staffs?' One of the other elders asked when he was out of sight.

Milly saw Oleander hesitate.

'We did find them,' she said finally. 'But... well... some of the temple mice have been using them.'

'What?' Spluttered one of the elders, Milly thought it was Chestnut. 'But that's dangerous – they're not trained.'

'I know,' Dan cut in. 'But it was the only way we could shift enough mice up here to fight the rats and free you.'

'Oh – I see,' said Chestnut. 'Then I suppose the risk was worth it.'

'But they need to give the staffs back now before they hurt themselves,' another elder whittered.

Milly thought it would be better for the staffs to stay where they were, with mice that could do something useful with them.

But Oleander nodded to the elder and then Dan called out to a passing mouse. 'Can you go and find Humble, Berry and Lichen and ask them to bring their staffs here?'

A few minutes later the three mice came running up.

'What's the problem?' Puffed Humble.

Dan sighed. 'I'm sorry – but you need to return the staffs to their rightful owners.'

Humble beamed. 'Great – glad to get rid of it – get's in the way all the time.'

He held out his staff and the elders all peered at it.

'The staff of making!' Squeaked Damson, and gently took it back.

Berry and Lichen weren't as keen as Humble to give theirs back – but they held them out reluctantly.

Acorn recognised his staff and immediately grabbed it back, but Chestnut noticed the reluctance of the temple mice – and as he took his staff he spoke to them. 'Have you enjoyed using the staffs?'

Both Berry and Lichen nodded.

Chestnut looked up and down the length of his staff.

'You've looked after them well,' he said. 'And we've just lost one of our apprentices. So, we may have a vacancy if one of you is interested in training to become an elder.'

Milly saw both mice glance at each other. She could see they were torn because only one of them could take up the offer. But then Dan interrupted.

'Actually,' he said. 'I've decided to give up my apprenticeship. So you have two vacancies.'

Chestnut peered at Dan in shock.

'Are you sure sure? I didn't think you were the sort of mouse who gave up easily...' But then his words faltered as he noticed the stone around Dan's neck, and after a moment he nodded his head.

'I see you've found a different destiny,' he breathed. 'A

greater one, perhaps.'

Chestnut turned back to Berry and Lichen. 'If you want you can both become new apprentices.'

The two mice nodded so much that it seemed their heads might fall off. Chestnut smiled at them. 'Good. That's settled, then. Now come with us.'

Chestnut and Damson turned and headed for the doorway that led inside the temple, with Berry and Lichen following.

'Looks like I've lost my two best guards,' Humble muttered to himself.

'One day they'll make great elders,' said Dan.

Humble laughed and pointed at the stone around Dan's neck. 'Just like one day you'll make a great king.'

Dan looked embarrassed. He wasn't trying to be a king. He glanced at Oleander. 'We don't need a king, we already have a queen.'

'Oh, I think I could share,' Oleander said with a smile.

Mordred had always liked to plan ahead.

The Weasel had only asked Mordred to march to the mountain and take over the bridge so that no one could escape. But Mordred had never really trusted that skinny mouse Hawthorn or believed in his plan to blow up the mountain. So, rather than just bring a small part of his army, he'd decided to bring the whole thing... all of his rat soldiers, the whole entourage needed to support them, and all of their equipment too.

And it turned out that was good planning, because now he had certain items with him that might be useful for, say, attacking a castle, or in this case, a temple.

Down on the road close to the town great wagons creaked to a halt and bits of wood and metal of all sizes and shapes were unloaded and laid out on the ground by strong rat soldiers. Then other rats with toolbelts and pencils behind their ears started unfolding plans and bolting the bits together.

Mordred watched as his war machines took shape, shouting at any rat he thought wasn't working fast enough. When it was getting dark a rat came up to him and saluted.

'What time should we stop for the night, sir?' He asked. His squad of rats had been grumbling for the last two hours that they were hungry.

'Stop?' Mordred jumped up in a rage. 'No-rat stops for food or sleep, I want the machines ready by the morning!'

The rat ran away out of range of any huge paws that might take a swipe at him and went back to his squad to tell them the bad news.

Hardly anyone slept well that night.

Down in the town any mice with windows high enough to see over the walls watched the burning fires and torches that lit up

Mordred's machines as they slowly took shape, wondering if the rats were going to use them to attack the town, or the temple.

Up in the temple nearly everyone was awake; Dan couldn't stop thinking about the temple stone and how he should be able to use it to save everyone; Lizzy spent the whole night roaming the temple, sure that big rat was still hiding somewhere; and Oleander lay in her bed worrying about Dan doing something heroic and getting killed.

Milly had fallen asleep okay to start with, completely exhausted by all the fighting, and was having a lovely dream. She was back at home, eating lovely cat food that had come out of a tin, but then her tummy growled and woke her up.

'Oh no, she breathed. 'I'm still here.'

And all she had to eat here was that awful dried fish. She was so disappointed that she got up and went for a walk around the temple. And as she went her mind turned back to the problem of the rats outside – surely there must be some way to get rid of them.

On her walk, Milly came across Lizzy, still looking for Mordred. 'Hello Lizzy.'

Lizzy nodded back and burped by mistake, and a little red flame and a puff of smoke came out in a mini explosion.

The sight made an idea pop into Milly's head, and she stopped and thought about it for a moment. It was crazy, but it was the first idea she'd had that felt like it might work.

She would just need some paper and a pencil.

19

Milly's clever plan

The next morning, as the sun peeped over the side of the mountain, Humble found Milly up on the temple walls scribbling on a piece of paper.

'Couldn't sleep?' He asked.

'No,' Milly replied as she held up her paper and compared it to the view in front of her. It was a map of the space in front of the temple, showing the road going down to the crossroads and beyond, and with all the nearby trees or bushes drawn in as well. Next to some she had added little x's, each with a different number against them.

'What's that for?' Asked Humble. Milly folded the paper up.

'Just an idea, probably not a very good one,' she said.

She looked up again at the view. Wisps of mist hovered just above the ground and shimmered in the rays of the early morning sun. Most of the rats had moved away from the temple sometime during the night, and only a few small groups were keeping watch. Maybe they were were giving up and leaving – she hoped so.

Then something moved down near the town, lurching into view from behind a rise in the ground. She saw rat soldiers pulling it forwards using long ropes, with more of them pushing it from behind. It looked like a wooden tower.

'What's that?' She asked, pointing.

Humble was watching it too.

'Trouble,' he said, and hurried away.

A few minutes later he came back with Dan and Oleander, and by that time the tower had reached the crossroads and turned up towards the temple. Now it was nearer Milly could see it was a made of a network of wooden beams with ladders up the sides, and it sat on fat wooden wheels that allowed it to be moved along.

Behind it were two other towers pulled by more rats.

'What are they for?' Asked Milly.

'To get onto our walls,' said Humble. 'And to protect them from arrows while they're doing it.'

'The staff of conquest would have smashed them to bits,' muttered Dan. He wished he had been able to catch Hawthorn when he'd had the chance and taken the staff from him.

All the staffs had different powers, but the temple stone was meant to combine them all. He should be able to use it to do whatever the staff of conquest could have done. But while Dan could feel its magic, he just didn't know how to use it.

Oleander took his paw and squeezed it. He knew she could

sense what he was thinking.

'I'll stop them somehow,' he promised her.

As the towers rumbled closer to the temple, Milly whispered something to Oleander. Oleander nodded and then spoke to Dan.

'Milly has an idea she wants to talk to me about.'

Dan shrugged and nodded. He thought Milly was a clever cat, but this was war. What did a fluffy cat know about that? 'I'll stay here, I need to see what they're up to.'

Oleander and Milly went to talk about her idea, while Dan and Humble stayed to watch the towers continue slowly up the road.

Dan went to find Milly and Oleander about an hour later. They were sitting with Lizzy next to one of the courtyard walls.

'Mordred and his men are right outside now, with those towers not far from the walls,' he said. 'I think Oleander should shift both of you away from here – down to the town where you'll be safer.'

'No,' said Oleander and Milly together.

But then there was a huge crash in the courtyard. A massive rock had fallen from the sky and made a dent in the ground before rolling a couple of times and stopping.

'Goodness!' Cried Oleander, jumping up.

'You see, it's not safe here, you must get out!' Dan said before running off.

Milly jumped up and followed Oleander as she ran after Dan up onto the walls.

The towers were very close now, no more than fifty paces away, ready to be pushed forward so that rats could climb up them. Behind the towers and further away was another wooden machine with a long arm. Small rat figures were winding back the arm as Milly watched. That had to be the machine that had thrown the rock.

Milly pulled out her piece of paper and drew in the towers and the throwing machine, then nudged Oleander and showed it to her. Oleander held up the map so she could compare it to the view in front of the temple. Then after a few moments she nodded to Milly and turned away to run back down the steps to the courtyard.

A big voice boomed from outside the walls. 'Are you ready to surrender?'

It was Mordred, standing beside one of his towers, just out of arrow range.

Dan shouted back. 'Never, I will destroy your towers with the power of the temple stone!'

Milly could see him concentrating, and the stone around his neck suddenly gleamed with white light. Had he worked out how to use its magic? Could he destroy the towers?

Dan held out his paws and the white light from the stone

flowed between them to create a glowing ball. When it was so intense Milly could hardly look at it, Dan threw the ball away from him, towards the tower next to Mordred.

The light soared out like a rocket and all the soldier rats ducked. It twizzled around in the air trailing smoke and then struck the top of the tower. A piece of wooden railing broke off and fell to the ground.

Mordred watched it fall. The rat soldiers stood up straight again.

'Is that it?' Mordred shouted. Some of the rats laughed.

Milly saw Dan try to concentrate again, but this time the stone wouldn't flare up at all. More of the rats started laughing.

Oh well... she supposed it was her turn now.

'No!' Shouted Milly. 'That is not it!'

'Oh, is that the cat again,' called out Mordred in a pretend-scared voice. 'And what are you going to do this time?'

She held one paw up high above her head. 'Use this!'

'Ooooh!' Mordred said sarcastically. 'A fluffy paw!

'This isn't just an ordinary paw – it's my paw of destruction!'

Laughter rippled back and forwards across the ranks of rat soldiers.

Dan glanced round at her. 'What are you doing?'

'This is my plan,' she hissed back.

'Pretending to have a paw of destruction?'

Milly shrugged. The way he said it made it sound silly. But maybe not for long. She pointed her paw dramatically at a clump of trees away to the left of the road.

Whhhooooffff! They burst into flames.

The rats' laughing died away as bits of burning twigs and leaves floated down onto their heads.

Dan stared at Milly in shock. 'How did you do that?'

No time to explain. She was counting in her head. When she got to ten, she moved her paw to point at big thicket of bushes on the hillside climbing up towards the top of the mountain.

Whhhooooffff! That went up in flames too.

She moved her paw slowly around, as though she was choosing where to point it next. Rats threw themselves to the ground whenever it seemed the paw was pointing at them. Milly kept counting in her head and, when she reached ten again, she thrust her paw out to point at the throwing machine at the back of Mordred's army. It exploded in a whoosh of fire, showering flaming splinters of wood onto the heads of the rats nearby, then lurched onto its side and flung a huge rock whistling at head height over Mordred's army. Rats in its path threw themselves to the ground and the rock finally thudded into the wooden tower next to Mordred. The tower trembled but stayed upright. Dan and the temple mice groaned, if only it had fallen over!

Milly used her paw of destruction to rub her whiskers. She knew what she was going to point at next but wanted to keep the rats guessing. Thank goodness that rock hadn't knocked the tower over...

She counted under her breath ... eight... nine... ten. Then pointed her paw suddenly at the tower.

For a moment nothing happened, and then a mass of smoke and fire burst out from the tower's base.

Mordred was close to the tower when it went up in flames and scrambled away from it brushing at his fur where sparks had singed it. How was that cat doing this? When had here ever been such a thing as a magic cat? But she seemed more powerful than Hawthorn! Maybe even than the Weasel.

Then, through a gap in the billowing smoke, he saw the cat up on the temple wall point her paw straight at him!

No way!

He leapt sideways and ran, dodging between squads of rats, scared that at any moment he would get blasted too.

He didn't care about the temple anymore, or about Hawthorn and that Weasel. He just wanted to to get as far away from here as he could.

Milly watched the rat army run away, following their leader down the slopes of the mountain towards the long bridge across the valley. It wasn't long before they were just dots in the distance.

She could hardly believe her plan had worked!

Dan was next to her, also staring at the retreating rats. 'How did you do that, Milly? I thought you couldn't do any magic.'

Milly kept peering into the distance. 'I can't. It wasn't me that blew all those things up, it was Oleander and Lizzy.'

But where were they? They should be back by now.

Milly glanced down into the courtyard, but couldn't see them anywhere. She ran to the nearest set of steps and bounded down them.

Dan followed Milly, starting to realise the terrible risk Oleander must've taken.

Queens! They just didn't seem to realise they should stay somewhere safe and leave the fighting to mice who were trained for it.

As he got down into the courtyard he saw the air shimmer near one of the walls and Oleander and Lizzy appear. The lizard looked wobbly on her legs, and she sank down onto the ground and curled into a ball. Oleander's fur was singed and covered in black soot. Dan ran to her and grabbed her in a big hug. 'What did you do?'

Oleander gently pulled herself free and walked over to Lizzy. 'I didn't do much... Lizzy did all the work, and I think she's exhausted.' She stroked the lizard's head, who grunted and closed her eyes.

Oleander looked up, searching around for Milly.

'Did it work?' She asked.

The cat was jumping up and down with excitement. 'Yes, it

did! You were great, and so brave. Thank goodness you're both okay.'

Dan cut in. 'Will someone tell me what's going on?'

'Well,' said Oleander. 'It should be Milly that tells you, it was all her idea.'

Dan turned to Milly.

'Well,' she started. 'Since some of the rats already thought I was a magical cat, what with the orb-thing and all, I thought I might be able to scare them away if they thought I had some even greater magic.'

'But you don't!'

Oleander cut in. 'No, she doesn't – but let her tell the story.' She nodded for Milly to go on.

'Well, I knew Lizzy could blow things up with her fire... and I wondered we could trick the rats by having someone shift her around outside in secret, and then have her blow things up when I pointed at them with my paw.'

'So you could pretend this was all happening because of your great magical powers?' Dan was catching on now. 'But how did you know where to point your paw?'

Oleander pulled a battered and singed piece of paper from a pouch in her belt and showed it to him. 'Look, Milly planned it all out.'

Dan took the piece of paper. It was a rough pencil map, showing trees and clumps of bushes and the road outside the temple. There was an 'x' with the number 1 against one stand of trees, and another 'x' with a 2 by a clump of bushes. He was getting the idea of this... he looked for another 'x' with a 3 against it and found it next to a hastily added drawing of the throwing machine. Okay... and then the 'x' with a 4... yes, against a scruffy drawing of the tower near the walls.

Oleander was pointing over his shoulder at the x's. 'I just had to shift to each of the x's in number order so that Lizzy could blast whatever was there – moving every ten seconds.'

Dan looked up into Oleander's eyes. 'That was very dangerous. What if the rats had seen you? What if they'd hurt you?'

'Don't be silly... the trees and the bushes were easy, there was no one there' Oleander replied. 'But we arrived a bit early at the throwing machine and some of the soldiers fired arrows at us while I was still counting to ten.'

She shrugged as though that was nothing. 'But they missed, and once they saw Lizzy blow up the machine they ran away. The tower was the biggest challenge, Lizzy was running out of fire, and I didn't want to get there early because of all the rats that were there, so I shifted Lizzy to it at the very last moment and she had to use every last bit of her fire.'

Dan hugged her again.

'Thank goodness you're all right,' he said. 'But you are the queen, you should have let someone else shift Lizzy'.

Oleander stood back and looked at him sternly. 'Milly wanted someone else to do it, but I insisted. I am the best one here at shifting, and Lizzy wouldn't have done it for anyone else,' she held her head a little higher. 'And in any case, you are right. I am the queen, and everyone here is my responsibility, and that means I should join in the fighting as best I can to protect them.'

Humble had come down from the walls and heard what had happened. He bowed. 'Now that's what I call a proper queen!'

Oleander was surprised when all the mice nearby started bowing down as well. She waved her paw towards Milly. 'I couldn't have done it without a really clever cat.'

20

Back Home at Last

Milly was falling through the air again. There were no clouds this time to get her wet, and below her woods and hills and a river spread in a huge expanse. Dan had explained her world was so far away it was too dangerous to shift straight onto the ground, and it was much safer to appear way up in the sky and then choose a place they could see and shift again.

Wind flattened her fur and whistled in her ears; it didn't seem safer to her. She spread out her paws in a star shape and circled slowly around and around. She couldn't help but worry that she would just keep on falling, until the ground below jumped up to splatter her into a cat pancake.

Roarrr! A billow of flames was lost in the air above. Milly looked over to where Lizzy was falling as well. She wasn't enjoying the experience very much either.

Clinging to the fur on Milly's back was Dan, while holding on tight to the scales around Lizzy's neck was Oleander.

'Can you see your house?' Shouted Dan.

Milly's eyes watered as she looked down, making it hard to

pick out anything in detail.

'No!'

'What about the river?'

Milly could see a river that meandered along the bottom of a valley. She could just make out a footbridge that crossed over it... was that the one down the hill from her house?

'Yes!' She shouted.

'We can't wait any longer... concentrate on somewhere there and we'll shift down... and don't forget to think about landing softly!' Dan shouted.

Milly concentrated.

'Three... two... one,' Dan counted down, waving with his paw so Oleander could see what number he had got to.

'Zero!'

Milly bumped onto the ground.

'Ouch!' It wasn't a soft landing. But at least it was a landing.

Lizzy appeared next to her, landing much more gently. Milly decided that Oleander was a lot better at this than Dan.

Oleander and Dan jumped down to the ground and hugged each other. They seemed to be doing a lot of that lately.

Milly looked around. They were in a field next to a river. She recognised it! She was home! From here it was only a five-minute walk up the hill to the house where she lived. No one was around, but some sheep were watching them curiously and munching grass at the same time.

'Are we near your home, Milly?' Asked Oleander.

Milly nodded, suddenly sad to have to say goodbye to her friends. It had been such an adventure it didn't seem quite real now that it was over and nothing dangerous was about to happen.

'Thanks for helping us, Milly,' said Dan. 'You saved us all from Mordred.'

'It's a shame he got away,' said Milly, wondering what mischief he would get up to once he had got over his defeat.

'And that Hawthorn,' added Dan.

'Do you think they'll be back?' Asked Milly.

'I'm sure they will,' said Dan.

'Well, if you need help,' said Milly. 'You know where I live.'

She didn't really mean that, but it felt like the right thing to say.

'Thank you, Milly,' said Oleander.

They all went quiet for a second.

'Well, I suppose I should go home,' said Milly.

Oleander hugged her paw.

'Goodbye Milly,' she said. 'And thanks again.'

'Yes, thanks,' said Dan, hugging her other paw.

Milly took her paws back and started heading up the hill, turning around a couple of times to wave. The mice watched until she hopped over a wall and went out of sight.

Oleander turned to Dan. 'Will she be all right?'

'I don't know, Mordred knows where she lives.'

'I wish we could do something to protect her.'

Lizzy nudged Oleander with her head, and started hopping up and down and pointing with one claw in the direction Milly had gone.

'Does she want to go with Milly?' Wondered Dan.

Lizzy nodded her head.

'Oh,' said Oleander. 'Do want to protect her?'

Lizzy nodded again.

Oleander was a bit upset that Lizzy wanted to stay here, but she had a feeling they'd all be meeting again soon. And Milly had done so much for them, she deserved to be kept safe.

'All right,' said Oleander. 'Off you go.'

The lizard nuzzled her head again and, without a glance at Dan, scampered off after Milly.

'I'll come and visit!' Called Oleander.

Then Lizzy was out of sight too.

'We should get back, there's lots to do,' said Dan.

'Yes,' agreed Oleander. They held paws and concentrated for a moment, then the air shimmered and they disappeared.

Milly was very excited to get home. She started to run when she saw her house, and when she got there, she jumped up onto the fence in one leap. The garden was empty, so she balanced along the fence to the end and then jumped down.

'Not so fast!' Came a nasty voice. Stripy was sitting under a bush in one of the flowerbeds. He slinked out onto the grass and stretched. 'I thought eventually you'd come back, although I was starting to wonder if you'd really run away for good.'

'Yeah, run away like a scaredy cat,' another voice came from behind her. 'Scared of what would happen to you.'

She glanced round and saw another cat, skinny and a bit stinky, slinking out from behind the dustbins.

Before she knew it, she was surrounded by all the cats from Stripy's gang.

'Someone's promised us a good reward to make you disappear,' Stripy purred.

Someone like Mordred, thought Milly, or maybe Hawthorn. She shivered and her fur fluffed up.

Tension grew in the air. The cats crept closer. There was nowhere to run!

Then there was a scrambling noise from the fence behind her and a scaly head poked over.

Lizzy? What was she doing here?

The lizard pulled herself up onto the top of the fence, teetered for a second, then jumped down into the garden.

'What on earth is that?' Gasped Stripy.

Milly smiled. She didn't know why Lizzy had suddenly appeared, but she was glad she had. Stripy and his gang were in for a bit of a surprise.

'Stripy,' she said. 'Say hello to my new friend Lizzy.'

The End

Printed in Great Britain
by Amazon

14451948R00140